What the critics are saying…

5 Angels and a Recommended Read "Whenever I pick up a N.J. Walters story, I always have high expectations, and yet, time and again, Ms. Walters surpasses those expectations to create a story that is erotic, unique, and truly touching." ~ *Fallen Angel Reviews*

"Passionate, emotional and sinfully entertaining, Katie's Art of Seduction is a delicious erotic romance that is sure to please readers of the genre. Get your copy today." ~ *Romance Reviews Today*

5 Stars "Katie's Art of Seduction is one of those rare stories that move you to strong emotions…Few books make me cry or laugh out loud, this is one of them." ~ Just Erotic Romance

5 Cupids "Ms. Walters entices her readers with a dark charismatic hero and a charming heroine. Her gift for alluring details is adding to the sensual world of light and darkness she has created in this story and making it all the more irresistible." ~ *Cupid's Library Reviews*

N.J. Walters

KATIE'S *Art*
Seduction

AWAKENING DESIRES

ELLORA'S CAVE
ROMANTICA PUBLISHING

An Ellora's Cave Romantica Publication

www.ellorascave.com

Katie's Art of Seduction

ISBN # 1419952536
ALL RIGHTS RESERVED.
Katie's Art of Seduction Copyright© 2005 N.J. Walters
Edited by: Pamela Cohen
Cover art by: Syneca

Electronic book Publication: March, 2005
Trade paperback Publication: September, 2005

Excerpt from *Erin's Fancy* Copyright © N.J. Walters, 2005

Warning:

The following material contains graphic sexual content meant for mature readers. *Katie's Art of Seduction* has been rated *E-rotic* by a minimum of three independent reviewers.

Ellora's Cave Publishing offers three levels of Romantica™ reading entertainment: S (S-ensuous), E (E-rotic), and X (X-treme).

S-*ensuous* love scenes are explicit and leave nothing to the imagination.

E-*rotic* love scenes are explicit, leave nothing to the imagination, and are high in volume per the overall word count. In addition, some E-rated titles might contain fantasy material that some readers find objectionable, such as bondage, submission, same sex encounters, forced seductions, etc. E-rated titles are the most graphic titles we carry; it is common, for instance, for an author to use words such as "fucking", "cock", "pussy", etc., within their work of literature.

X-*treme* titles differ from E-rated titles only in plot premise and storyline execution. Unlike E-rated titles, stories designated with the letter X tend to contain controversial subject matter not for the faint of heart.

Also by N.J. Walters:

Annabelle Lee
Harker's Journey
Erin's Fancy

Katie's Art of Seduction

Awakening Desires

Dedication

Thank you to my husband, Gerard, for his continued support, advice, love, and encouragement. Also, thanks to Pamela, as always for her hard work, guidance, and belief in me and my stories.

Prologue

She emerged silently from the shadows. One minute he lay in solitary splendor on his enormous bed, and the next he sensed he was no longer alone. As she drifted across the room to stand at the foot of the bed, her pale skin glowed in the faint light from the window. He felt no surprise at her unexpected appearance. Rather, a feeling of anticipation rose within him. What would she do?

Her hands slid down her body and his eyes followed her every move as she lifted the hem of her silky gown and leisurely pulled it over her head. Flinging the covering away, she stood with her feet spread apart, daring him to look his fill. Tempting him.

His gaze flowed over her small, but well-shaped breasts, down her torso and over her legs that were long and lithe, perfect for wrapping around his waist as he thrust into her, and he would thrust into her. She had a runner's build, sleek yet strong, and he sensed she was more than capable of taking his weight in bed.

"Come." His voice was harsh and thick with desire as he held his large, rough hand out towards her. He sat with his back propped against several pillows and the black satin sheet riding low around his waist.

At eight inches over six feet and more than two hundred and fifty pounds of solid muscle, he knew he was an intimidating sight. Scars radiated out from beneath an eyepatch, which covered his ruined left eye and ran down the side of his face. But his features were veiled by the shadows of the night and for that he was thankful.

His hand never wavered, but remained extended towards her. "Come."

Her hands gripped the bottom of the bed and she used it as leverage to pull her legs up behind her. She had poised herself at the end of the bed, sitting on her knees with her hands braced on the sheets in front of her.

His hand remained extended, but his fingers curled slightly, beckoning her to him. Their combined breathing was the only sound in the room. Hers — short and shallow. His — long and deep. He waited.

The sheets rustled sensually as she inched towards him. His patience was rewarded when her smaller, softer hands covered his. As he watched her, she kissed the palm of his hand and placed it on her chest. Her heart beat a frantic rhythm but there was no hesitation in her actions.

Sliding his hand to one side, she covered her small but well-shaped breast with it and rubbed herself against his palm. The taut nipple stabbed the center of his palm. The erotic picture she made as she pleasured herself with his hand captivated him.

Dropping his hand to her hip, he urged her closer. Eagerly, she crawled over him until she was seated on his thighs facing him. He framed her face with his hands and held her easily. "Don't make me have to ask you twice." She tried to lean forward to kiss him, but he held her in place, waiting for her agreement.

She went still in his arms, licking her lips nervously. "I won't."

He nodded, satisfied that she understood he would brook no disobedience in the bedroom. She sat quietly in his grasp, even as her hips slowly swayed back and forth seeking his erection. He smiled, pleased with her.

Dropping his hands from her face, he slid them up her sleek thighs, over her full hips and slender waist, finally coming to rest on her breasts. She sighed in relief as he palmed them both, taking his time to test their plump weight and velvety texture with his hands before allowing his thumbs to brush her already tight nipples.

"More." Her voice was a seductive whisper in the darkness.

"More," he agreed. Using his finger and his thumb, he lightly pinched her nipples. She moaned again in response, and he could feel the heat of her against his rigid cock. Her fingers dug into his scalp, urging him on.

She was an aphrodisiac. Her every move, every sound, made him harder. Her response was immediate and intoxicating to him. The hunter in him wanted to pounce and drag her body beneath him. Soon, he promised himself.

"Put your hands behind your head," he commanded.

Slowly, she released her grip on his hair and shifted her hands until they were behind her neck. He positioned her to his liking, spreading her elbows as wide as they would go before he was satisfied, the pose thrusting her breasts forward.

Trailing his fingers over the sensitive skin of her inner arms, he was rewarded when she shivered in delight. His lips followed the path of his fingers and he tasted her skin, tugging it gently between his teeth and then soothing the slight sting with his tongue.

His tongue traced its way across her collarbone and then around her breasts until they were both glistening and wet. Testing the fullness of her breasts, he plumped them up in his hands and then carefully took one of her nipples between his teeth.

"Oh, yes," she cried.

He could tell she was tempted once to move her arms, but when he pulled back slightly, she pushed them back and thrust *her breasts higher to appease him. His cock flexed, eagerly seeking her moist heat. Her hips rocked restlessly against him. Seeking relief.*

Shifting her slightly, he adjusted her until her hips were pressed against his straining erection. Grinding herself against him, she rode his cock, her hands still locked behind her head. Her breasts bounced and jiggled as she rocked.

He felt his own control begin to slip and grabbed her hips to stop her. She fought his control, but he wouldn't be denied. "Be still," he ordered.

She quivered with indecision for a moment before settling quietly against his rock-hard cock.

"You look so beautiful just sitting there awaiting my pleasure." He anchored her hips with his hands and lifted her slightly off his body. "You'll like what comes next."

He slid down in the bed until he was lying flat against the pillows, and then pulled her up until she was straddling his face. Open for his inspection, he reached out his fingers and gently touched the pale pink flesh of her sex. It was soft, wet and glistening. The scent of her arousal filled his nostrils as he breathed in her sexual perfume. His cock twitched.

"Hold on to the headboard," he ordered as he positioned her for his comfort. Her hands immediately wrapped around the wood and she whimpered in anticipation. She was open completely to his mouth and hands.

"You look delicious," he whispered. Nuzzling her soft pubic hair with his nose, he found the hard nubbin of flesh between her legs and tongued it briefly before moving on to lap at the sweet pink flesh of her sex.

He indulged himself to his heart's content, licking and sucking, while enjoying her moans and pleas for more. But he was ruthless and held her hips in his large hands so that she got only as much pleasure as he wanted to give her.

His tongue slid around her moist opening and he drove it inside of her, pulling her against his face as he did. Working her with his tongue, he used his fingers to play with her hard little clit. She was frantic now. Her hips slammed against his face until she gave one long cry and her inner muscles convulsed. He felt her wetness on his face and in his mouth as she came.

Laughing, he pulled her down alongside him until her face was next to his. "Taste how good you are." His tongue traced her lips until they opened and her tongue darted out to lick at his lips and face. Driving his tongue into her mouth, he captured hers and claimed it as his.

She belonged to him. All of her. Body and soul.

Not breaking the kiss, he sat up with her in his arms. Pushing the sheet down his body, he bared himself to her. Tasting her lips for one last time, he whispered against them. "Taste me." Then he lay back down in the shadows and left her sitting there above him.

His cock was hard and thick as it extended upward from his body. Parting her lush lips, she went down on him. Circling the top of his shaft with her tongue, she laughed with delight when a pearly drop of fluid seeped to the tip. Licking it up with her tongue, she held it there suspended for a moment before swallowing it. His hands fisted in the sheets.

When her wet mouth descended upon his cock again, he almost shot off the bed. Nibbling her way down his length and then back up again, she teased him mercilessly before finally taking the tip in her mouth. Rolling her tongue around the bulbous tip, she sucked it like a candy as she swirled it in her mouth.

Taking him deep into her mouth, she allowed his length to slide against her teeth. Her tongue traced the protruding vein as she slid his cock in and out of her mouth in an almost hypnotic rhythm. He thrust his hips, wanting her to take more, and she instantly complied, taking him deeper than he thought possible. His fingers entangled in her hair, holding him to her.

Enthusiastically, she licked and sucked as she straddled his thigh. Spreading her legs wider, she rubbed her mound against his hair-roughened leg. Her sweat-covered skin slid easily against him. She moaned as she pleasured herself, almost causing him to come with the vibrations of her own gratification.

Her fingers were never still as they shaped and cupped his testicles. Her nails teased the bottom of his shaft as her teeth and tongue played with the rest of his cock. He could feel his balls tightening and knew that his own release was close.

He was torn between wanting to be inside her and wanting to let her suck him to completion. "I want to come inside you," he said in a hoarse groan.

Suddenly, he wanted – no, needed – to say her name. "Tell me your name." Until he knew it, he knew he couldn't possess her totally. "What's your name?" His voice shook with rising anger at her refusal to tell him.

As if she hadn't heard him, she doubled her efforts, continuing to pleasure him until her name no longer mattered. Nothing mattered but the pleasure she was giving him. He could feel his orgasm rising within him like a living beast. From deep inside him, it rose with such power that he thought it would go on forever. The hot seed erupted from him, spreading across his stomach and chest.

"No." He awoke on a cry of anguish, sitting straight up in bed before falling back against the pillows on a groan of despair. The wetness on his stomach made him feel like a twelve-year-old boy again, helpless and weak. He loathed the feeling.

Throwing his arm over his face, he took a deep breath trying to calm his erratic breathing. His lungs were working like a bellows, his body was covered in sweat, and his long hair was plastered to his skull and neck. He shivered slightly as he lay there trying to recover.

His lovely nymph, who had been haunting his dreams of late, was gone.

Disgusted with himself, he threw back his plain cotton sheets and dragged himself out of bed. He gave a snort of laughter as he remembered the satin sheets in the dream. That should have been a dead giveaway that it was only a dream. He might have money, but he still wasn't a satin sheet kind of guy. Big and rough, he needed belongings that would hold up to hard use.

He padded into the adjoining bathroom, not bothering with the lights, and turned the shower on cold. Ducking beneath the cold spray, he soaped himself from head to toe and then rinsed off. Two minutes later, he flipped off the water and snagged a towel. Rubbing it over his still sensitive body was almost an act of torture. Swearing, he flung the towel away and stalked naked out the door, through the bedroom, and down the hall to his office.

The carpet muffled the sound of his feet as he all but stomped to the corner of the room. He knew it was there. Waiting.

The click of the light as he turned it on was as loud as a gunshot against the quiet of the night. The light, though dim, forced him to blink several times before he could focus on the picture. On her. His hands clenched into fists as he stepped back from the painting.

Pulled by equal but conflicting desires, he sank down into a leather chair, his gaze never leaving the painting. While half of him wanted to fling the object against the wall and destroy it, the other half burned with the desire to possess the woman portrayed in it.

The sound of toenails clicking on the hardwood floor broke the silence. A moment later his wolfhound, Gabriel, thrust his head onto his lap. "I didn't mean to disturb you," he murmured. He absently rubbed the dog's head and neck. Gabriel whimpered in doggy ecstasy, turning his head this way and that, making sure every spot received attention.

Eventually, Gabriel flopped on the floor next to him, content and ready to sleep again. The sound of their breathing was the only sound except for the occasional rumble of traffic. The night ticked on towards the dawn.

Staring at the painting, he waited. Eventually, his hands relaxed and he sank back into the comfort of the large chair and tilted his head back. With his eyes closed, he shook his head in disgust. He could no more destroy the painting than harm a hair on her head, this beautiful woman who now haunted his dreams with her tousled brown hair, expressive blue eyes, and incredibly sexy body. He could feel his dick stirring to life again. Just thinking about her made him hard.

From the moment he'd first laid eyes on the painting in the window of a little coffee shop, he'd had to own it. The beauty of the artist's work had caught his eye, but it was the subject that had captured his imagination. Now that he possessed the picture, he was filled with a yearning—no, a compulsion—to meet her. He felt connected to her somehow. There was a bond between them that he couldn't explain, but he had to find out what it was.

He rubbed his hands over his face and sighed. Maybe he'd just been working too damn hard lately, and that made him more susceptible to his dreams. He really didn't know and didn't care. Regardless, he didn't think the dreams would stop until he discovered what it was about her that fascinated him so. That meant he had to meet her.

Realistically, he expected the dreams to disappear the moment he met her. After all, she was just an ordinary woman, albeit a beautiful one, probably living a completely mundane life. The sexy goddess from his dreams was the perfect creation of his overworked mind. In his experience, people rarely lived up to his expectations.

Better to deal with it head-on so he could put it behind him, especially if he wanted another uninterrupted night's sleep. He was disturbed with how easily this unknown woman had slipped, uninvited, into his dreams. Being out of control was not a feeling he enjoyed.

With his usual take-charge style, he'd already set the wheels in motion and had begun the first step in the hunt. Find the artist and he'd find the woman in the painting.

The shadows were a light gray when he finally arose from the chair. Cold and stiff, he stretched for a moment to work the kinks out of his neck and shoulders. Gabriel raised his furry head for a moment, but seeing nothing wrong, returned to his doggy dreams.

Ignoring the dog, he slowly approached the picture for one last look. His finger traced the outline of her face before he made a sound of disgust and clicked off the light. It didn't help. He could still see her sitting on the crumbling stone steps of a city apartment building, gazing at the dawn. Her beguiling face was bathed in the morning light, and her lips curved upward in a secret smile. He blinked, but she still sat there. Waiting.

"I'll find you." It was both a threat and a promise that he left her with as he made his way back down the hall and to bed.

Chapter One

"I need a Caesar salad, two pasta salad specials and a chicken salad sandwich on multigrain." Katie clipped the orders to the board hanging just inside the kitchen door, and deftly scooped up the plates that waited on the counter. She didn't wait for a reply or even an acknowledgement. She knew that Lucas had heard her. He always did.

She smiled as she watched him work. Lucas Squires was her boss and friend. He owned this popular coffee shop, aptly named Coffee Breaks, where she had worked since she was fourteen. Lucas had started her in the kitchen washing dishes and helping prep for meals. He had taught her how to cook and then eventually, she moved out into the shop to waitress. The patrons were friendly and the tips were good, but most of all Katie felt at home here.

Bumping her hip against the swinging door, she swept back out of the kitchen and into the lunchtime fray. Her movements were smooth and economical as she placed orders in front of their rightful owners. She smiled and chatted as she dispensed coffee, tea, and cold drinks, all the while tempting her customers to try a double fudge brownie, a Napoleon, a strawberry tart, or some other delight from behind the bakery case for dessert. Many of the people she served were regular customers, people who worked in the office buildings a few blocks over who made the trek here once or twice a week because the food was excellent and the desserts were sublime.

Katie rang up sales, scooped up pastries and slices of pie for people to take home or back to the office, cleared tables, and collected smiles and tips in equal quantity. Katie had a natural friendly air about her that made people feel comfortable. She drew people to her with her easy smile and lively blue eyes. She had an unhurried manner about her that permeated the shop, giving the place a relaxed and cheerful atmosphere.

Katie glanced at the clock as the last lunchtime group, a table of five, left. A handful of customers were scattered around the shop, but everyone had their orders and were busy finishing their meals or sipping their coffee. It was just before two in the afternoon and the busiest part of the day was behind her. Between now and closing at six there would be a slow but steady stream of people who just wanted a coffee or a snack.

Sighing in relief, Katie stretched her arms over her head, the move accentuating her long, lean, athletic build. Standing five foot eight in her stocking feet, she was as comfortable with her size ten body as she was with her short brown hair, cut in a no-nonsense style. Katie wore no makeup and her morning routine consisted of a shower, moisturizer, and running her fingers through her hair. Her movements drew more than one appreciative male eye, but Katie never noticed.

"Is that it?"

Katie turned at the sound of Lucas's rough voice. She watched as he scanned the shop, missing nothing. "That's the end of the lunch crowd."

"Have Judy watch the counter." Lucas disappeared back into the kitchen.

Katie shook her head, amused at her boss's shorthand speech. "Judy, I'm out back talking to Lucas. Call if you need anything." One more glance reassured her that the teenage girl would be fine for a few minutes, so she poured herself a cup of iced tea and retreated to the sanctuary of the kitchen.

Standing in the doorway, she paused for a moment, and watched Lucas work. At forty, he was sixteen years her senior, but he'd always treated her like a younger sister. He was six feet tall, but looked much larger as he was built like a brick building, solid and unyielding. His face was a strong one, compelling, if not classically handsome with a nose that had been broken more than once. His blond hair was cut short and was not yet showing any signs of gray. Most customers would never have believed that it was this man who created the culinary treats that they purchased every day.

A tattoo peeked out from under the edge of his white t-shirt and Katie knew the barbed wire design ran all the way around his bicep. It was one of several he had, all reminders of his days in prison.

Behind his hard façade, Katie knew, lay one of the gentlest souls in the world. Lucas had discovered his skill at baking behind bars when at eighteen he'd gone to jail for severely beating a man. That he'd been protecting his mother from his abusive father at the time had not mattered to the courts. By the time he'd gotten out of prison several years later, his mother was dead and his father was doing time for the deed.

Katie walked over to him and leaned into his side. His arm automatically came around her shoulders. She was alone since the death of her beloved grandmother, Olivia, and though they were an unlikely pair, they were family by choice, if not by blood.

"Is everything all right?" Katie placed her glass on the counter and waited patiently.

"Yeah, for now." He gave her a quick squeeze before moving away from her. Opening the oven door, he checked the pies that were baking and then removed them, one by one, until all six of them were steaming on the counter. The air was filled with the smells of cherries, apples, and cinnamon.

He laughed when she breathed deeply and sighed, then deftly cut a piece of cherry pie and heaped it onto a plate. "Let it cool for a minute so you don't burn your tongue," he cautioned her as he handed her the plate.

Katie took the mouth watering piece of pie with one hand, and pulled open a drawer and dug out a fork with the other. Settling everything in front of her at the counter, she pulled over a stool and plunked herself down. "So what's up?" she asked as she broke off a flaky piece of pastry with her fork.

"I sold your painting."

Her pie lay forgotten as she stared at Lucas. The hum of the refrigerator was the only sound in the quiet kitchen other than the sudden ringing in her ears. Surely, she had misunderstood him. She opened her mouth to speak but nothing came out. Swallowing hard, she tried again. "But that was just for display in the shop." Her voice shook as badly as her hand, and she carefully laid her fork on the edge of the plate. The clink of stainless steel against the earthenware plate sounded unusually loud in the silence that followed.

Lucas just shook his head. They'd had this conversation before and he was continually frustrated by her insistence that she keep her talent a secret. "Your work is good enough to display, it's good enough to sell." His pale blue eyes studied her as he drew up another stool and sat next to her. "What are you waiting for, Katie? You can't stay here forever."

"Don't you want me here?" She felt lightheaded and slightly nauseous at the thought that Lucas might want her to go. Her hands grasped the edge of the counter for support.

"Honey, of course I want you here." He reached across the counter and took her pale, cool hand in his larger, warmer one. "But you're better than this place, Katie. You've got real talent." She stared at his familiar countenance, gauging the sincerity of his words. Lucas had never lied to her.

"I'm not ready to leave. I don't want to leave." Her voice was getting louder and more agitated as she spoke. Katie took a deep breath. Then another. It didn't help. Her heart continued to pound inside her chest, and the room seemed to spin around her.

"You don't have to go anywhere," Lucas soothed, his voice low and reassuring. "But I want you to consider letting me hang some of your work here. We could advertise it and have a small opening party here at the shop." Ruthlessly, he played his trump card. "It would be good for business."

Katie's thoughts continued to whirl. The painting had been a self-portrait of sorts. It was a side view of her, sitting on the stone steps of her apartment building, watching the sunrise over the city. She knew she'd captured the beauty of the moment as the colors of the morning sun had washed the aged buildings, making the old, decrepit neighborhood beautiful for that one moment of time.

"Who bought it?" Katie found it hard to imagine her painting hanging in some stranger's home.

Lucas shrugged, unconcerned by such details. "I don't know, really. Some businessman sent his assistant down to buy it. I told her it wasn't for sale." His eyes gleamed and a rare smile crossed his face. "Next thing I know she's on the cell phone and is offering me two thousand for it."

"Dollars?" Katie managed to sputter.

"Yeah, that was my reaction. I guess she took my shock for denial and offered three." Reaching into his apron pocket he withdrew a plain envelope. "I told her that the artist wanted thirty-five hundred in cash."

Katie's hand shook as she reached out and took the envelope. She opened it and just stared at the contents as they slid out of her nerveless fingers. A pile of fifties spilled onto the counter. Katie had never seen that much money at one time in her entire life.

Lucas pushed a small white square towards her. "The lady left her card and asked to be informed if the artist were ever to have a showing."

"All that money…" Katie shook her head slowly in disbelief, totally at a loss for words.

Lucas laughed and scooped her off her seat and swung her around in a tight circle. "Katie, this is your dream come true. This proves that you're a real artist and can make a living doing what you love." Lucas continued to twirl her about until she was dizzy.

"But, I don't want to leave here." Taking a quick, surveying glance around the coffee shop and then back to

Lucas, she suddenly felt a little sadness mixed with her joy. She clung to Lucas's strong shoulders for support. Her head was spinning and he was the grounding for her world.

Gently, he lowered her feet to the floor and steadied her with his strong, capable hands. His ice-blue eyes never left hers as he sought to reassure her. "You don't have to leave. At least not right away." He placed his finger over her mouth before she could protest. "You owe it to yourself to try. I want you to be happy, and if you're honest with yourself, this is what you've always wanted. This is why you've taken art classes at night since you were sixteen."

Katie nodded, unable to be anything but honest with Lucas. "I know," she whispered.

"Think about it. We'll talk more in a few days." He guided her back to her stool and, when she was seated, handed her the fork she had discarded earlier. "Now eat your pie and get back to work."

Katie dutifully ate the pie, but for once tasted nothing. It could have been sawdust she chewed instead of warm, sweet cherries and flaky pastry. Her gaze never left the pile of fifty-dollar bills that still lay on the counter. Her mind whirled with the possibilities. She could buy a lot of art supplies with that kind of money. For once, she had the money to try her hand at painting some really large canvases. Or maybe, she could actually go on a trip. A real vacation. She'd never been out of the city before and she longed to paint the countryside or the seashore.

The possibilities were limitless, but knowing her, she'd probably put most of it in the bank, and talk herself out of spending any of it. Well, she assured herself, she could probably talk herself into spending a few hundred bucks of it at the art supply store. It was an investment. Sort of.

Later that evening, Katie turned up the collar of her coat as she turned the key in the front door of Coffee Breaks. The wind had a bite to it on this cold February evening and Katie had stayed at the shop far later than she'd intended. Lucas would be angry with her if he knew she'd stayed this late. It had taken her much longer than usual to do her normal closing routine. Her mind had wandered to her painting and her sudden windfall, and somehow several hours had slipped by. It was only eight in the evening, but this time of year it was dark.

Pulling on the door to reassure herself that it was locked, Katie then dumped her keys in the pocket of her long, purple wool jacket and started walking briskly down the sidewalk. She tugged her scarf tighter around her neck, shifted her beat-up brown leather backpack to her right shoulder and then shoved her hands in her pockets for warmth. Cursing herself for forgetting her gloves this morning, she scanned the sidewalk as she went.

She wrapped her hand protectively around the envelope in her pocket as she scanned the sidewalk nervously. Katie scolded herself for not going to the bank earlier, but she'd been too dazed to think straight. And there was no way she was stopping at night to deposit this large a sum of money. First thing in the morning, she assured herself, it was straight to the bank on her way to work. In the meantime, the money would just have to be safe with her for one night.

Coffee Breaks was on the edge of a busy business district and was surrounded by much larger and taller office buildings. In comparison to its neighbors, it was housed in a relic from a bygone era, a three-story brick building that was slightly worn at the edges. The landlord did little to upkeep the building, but Lucas had repaired the area around the front of the shop. The sidewalk in front was always kept swept and, in the summer, tubs of bright flowers welcomed people inside. There were several apartments on each of the other two floors. The location was excellent and the rent was affordable.

Traffic was brisk, but there was no one else walking the street as she strode farther from the shop and closer to her apartment. Living only a fifteen minute walk from work was a bonus in the city and she saved quite a bit of money by walking. The business district gave way to an older residential area. The buildings were mostly brick, much of it chipped and crumbling, and no more than five or six stories high. A little worse for wear, but still affordable for those on a low income or pension.

It was really a small community within the larger city. In the summer, the sounds and smells of people cooking and living filled the air. Elderly men and women sat on balconies and front steps and chatted while children played on the sidewalks and in the empty lots around the neighborhood.

This time of year, everyone was inside and the street was unusually quiet. The buildings cast a menacing shadow onto the street and their lights were like eyes, watching her every step. Katie had always felt safe, but tonight she felt nervous. It was all that money, practically burning a hole in her pocket. It had to be. She'd walked this route for years, but tonight she wished she taken a cab.

"There's nothing to be afraid of," she muttered to herself even as she gripped her keys in her right hand and slowly withdrew them from her pocket. Scanning back and forth with her eyes, she kept walking briskly towards the next corner. Her leather hiking boots measured her steps as she strode down the sidewalk, their soles making a comforting thumping sound. Katie knew of people who'd gotten mugged in this part of town. It didn't happen often, but it did happen, especially at night. She stood tall and squared her shoulders. She would be no easy target.

A shuffling noise behind her made her stop and spin around. "Who's there?" she demanded. Her heart pounded as she balanced herself on her toes, ready to fight or run. A soft woof and the padding of feet answered her. Katie felt her tense muscles begin to relax until she saw the apparition rocketing out of the dark.

It was a dog. But not like any other she'd ever seen. It was huge and coming right for her with its mouth open and its tongue hanging out. Katie froze to the spot, not wanting to provoke any aggression. "Nice doggy," she soothed. "Don't eat me."

The large predator continued to charge straight for her, and Katie braced herself for attack. At the last moment, the huge animal skidded to a stop in front of her, planted its behind on the sidewalk, and held up its right front paw. Katie eyed the beast warily, but he continued to sit patiently with his paw raised.

Gingerly, she reached out and gave it one quick tug. "Pleased to meet you." Realizing what she'd just done, she groaned. "Now I'm talking to a dog."

Pleased with her response, the animal thrust his head under her hand and whined. Katie smiled in spite of herself, slipping her keys back in her pocket so she could rub his fur with both hands. "You're just a big baby, aren't you?" she crooned softly.

The dog whined and tilted his head to one side so she could scratch him there. Katie gave herself up to the pleasure of petting the gentle creature. This was no stray dog by any means. The dog was obviously well-fed, well-groomed, and well-behaved. Peering closely at his collar, she saw a tag. As she started to reach for it, the animal pulled away and started trotting down the sidewalk. When he was a few steps away from her, he turned and waited.

Katie laughed. "Going to walk me home, are you?" The dog woofed in response.

Checking her pocket to make sure the precious white envelope was still tucked safely away, she continued down the sidewalk. Her early nervousness had vanished with the arrival of this new friend. "So you're going to be mysterious and not let me know your name." The dog trotted beside her, his tail wagging happily behind him, unconcerned by her pronouncement.

Katie got a better view of him as they reached a well-lit intersection. If she wasn't mistaken this was some kind of wolfhound. Big and gray and very regal-looking. They crossed the street and Katie was relieved to see her building in the distance.

The old five-story relic might not be up to many people's standards, but it was sturdily built and fairly well-maintained. The brick had faded over time and was a washed-out pink, rather than red. The fire escape served as a patio and the elevator rarely worked. But the warm light shining from the windows was comforting as she hurried closer. This was the home she'd shared with her grandmother since her mother had left her there when Katie was only four. Now that her grandmother was gone, it was her home. This was where she belonged.

The dog kept pace with her as she quickened her step and sped towards home. She could see her breath as she hurried along and longed for the heat and comfort of her apartment. Safety was only a few steps away. Instinctively, her left hand clutched the envelope in her pocket even tighter. The loud crinkling noise sounded unusually loud to Katie and she forced her hand to relax its death grip on the money.

A car slowed down as it neared her, and Katie automatically moved to the middle of the sidewalk and away from the curb. She pulled her keys from her pocket and wielded them like a weapon. The dog silently slid to her left side, so it was between her and the vehicle. A low growl rumbled from the animal as it bared its teeth at the driver. The car sped up and quickly disappeared down the street. Katie stared at the dog in disbelief as he looked at her with a doggy grin on his face and his tongue hanging out. "Well, aren't you full of surprises!"

Katie felt nothing but relief as she climbed the slightly crumbling stone steps to her building and unlocked the door to the lobby. "Come on in," she invited the dog as she held the door open. "You can't stay out all night in this cold." The dog sat on the sidewalk in front of the building, in no hurry to go anywhere. Katie tried to coax him inside, but once again he ignored her efforts.

Suddenly, the dog's ears perked up and Katie heard a soft whistle. The dog immediately turned away and loped across the street and into the shadows. As she watched him disappear into the darkness, the feeling of being watched returned full force to Katie.

Quickly, she slammed the door to the building and looked out from the relative safety of the lobby. A huge shadow detached itself from the side of the building and moved away down the sidewalk and Katie watched in silence as the dog trotted happily beside it.

The moment they were swallowed up by the night, Katie became aware of her own vulnerability. Standing in the lobby, she was spotlighted for one and all to see. Gripping the envelope in one hand and her keys in the other, she raced up three flights of stairs and down the hall to her apartment.

She fumbled with the keys, almost dropping them, as she unlocked the door. It seemed to take forever, but finally she was inside. Her heart pounded a frantic rhythm in her chest as her mad dash up the stairs and her fear of a possible assailant caught up to her.

Katie's knees buckled and she sat down hard on the floor, propping her back against the locked door. Her breath came in harsh gasps and she forced herself to take deep breaths to calm herself. She hadn't been imagining things. Someone had followed her home.

Chapter Two

He hadn't meant to scare her. He'd simply wanted to catch a glimpse of her now that he knew she was real and not some figment of the artist's imagination. After his initial shock, Cain Benjamin had simply watched from the shadows as she talked to his dog. Gabriel had trotted happily at her side and Cain admitted to himself that he was jealous of his damned dog. He wanted to be the one walking beside her, sharing conversation and laughter. But that would probably never happen.

She'd known someone was watching her and that surprised him. Most people were very unaware of their surroundings. Maybe it was some intrinsic part of her personality that had been aware of him or at least sensed that someone was nearby.

He'd smelled her fear as she walked, but still, she hadn't run from it. She'd drawn herself up and pulled out her keys as a weapon to defend herself. He'd felt pride in her at that moment and knew he'd been right in assuming that she was special.

It had taken all the self-control he possessed not to scoop her up like some Neanderthal caveman and drag her back to his lair. His entire body was pulsing with need, and he clenched his teeth as he adjusted his cock to ease the ache.

Cain turned down an alley, automatically choosing the darkest route. The night was his friend, the shadows his companion. He knew his way unerringly around the city through all the back alleys and unlit lanes.

Unzipping his jacket, he welcomed the cold air on his overheated body. It helped. Barely. He concentrated on his breathing, taking one deep cleansing breath after another, as he desperately tried to put her out of his thoughts.

Twenty minutes later, with his body back under control, he crossed a deserted street and entered the darkness of the park. Cain stayed off the well-lit walking trails, confining his rambles to the dark grassy paths between the tall, mature trees. Their height and their branches sheltered him, even at this time of year when most of them were bare of leaves. Gabriel, who had quietly walked at his side, now started to whine softly.

"All right, boy." Cain's voice was a low rumble. Reaching into the pocket of his leather jacket, he withdrew a large piece of braided rope and threw it with all his might. Gabriel disappeared into the dark, barking happily as he ran. Seconds later, he reappeared and dropped the rope at Cain's feet.

Tug-of-war was next on Gabriel's agenda. It was amusing to watch his large, usually aristocratic dog, rolling and romping like a puppy. Gabriel raced around the dark field, barking and chasing the rope toy. About forty minutes later, when he'd had enough, Gabriel plopped down by his master's feet, puffing and panting with his exertions. Cain crouched down and absently rubbed the animal's belly. He usually enjoyed Gabriel's playtime, but tonight his mind was occupied. With her.

"Let's go home." Gabriel recognized the word "home" immediately and jumped to his feet, and trotted off down the path, rope toy dangling from his mouth, confident that Cain was behind him.

Cain stood more slowly, breathing in the crisp winter air as if it could somehow rejuvenate him. Rolling his shoulders to release some of the tension he felt, he ambled after Gabriel. His large boots crunched the snow beneath his feet as he wandered back onto the empty streets. He quickened his pace as Gabriel hurried on ahead of him.

Life was a predictable routine that had somehow felt restrictive ever since he'd bought that damn painting. For some unknown reason, he no longer seemed to fit in the life he'd created. Cain continued on, lost in his thoughts, mindlessly following the well-worn path that both man and dog trod nightly.

The world was truly a different place at night. It was harder to be alone in the summertime when more people were out enjoying the night air. In the winter, most people were tucked inside early and he could enjoy the solitude of the park. Tonight, thoughts of her filled his head.

It was one of those moments of fate that changed a person's life forever. Just a week ago, he hadn't known she existed. His life had been predictable. He had been content with things, if not particularly happy. On one of his nightly walks, he'd turned left instead of right and had been drawn to a painting in the window of a coffee shop. With both his large hands placed against the glass window, he'd stood transfixed by the sight. Never in his life had he wanted anything as badly as he'd wanted that painting or the woman in it.

Cain walked swiftly behind an impressive, stone six-story building. Reaching into his pocket he pulled out his keys and unlocked the large steel door in front of him. Gabriel trotted ahead of him as he paused to lock the door behind him. Crossing the private parking garage, his footsteps echoed in the cavernous space. A few well-placed security lights, gave him more than enough light to see while keeping the area largely in shadows. An elevator waited at the other end of the garage. He pressed the button and stepped inside when the door slid open. In silence, he and Gabriel rode to the top floor.

The elevator opened to a small dimly lit lobby. There was one more door to open and Cain sighed in relief when he closed and locked it behind him. Gabriel, unaffected by his master's pensive mood, abandoned his rope toy just inside the door, and headed to the kitchen for a snack. Cain dropped his keys on a small oak table just inside the door and hung his coat on the heavy mahogany coat rack next to it. The antique coat stand was almost as tall as he was and Cain had purchased it because he liked its smooth, simple lines and its heavy construction.

Cain ignored the living room that was straight ahead, turned to the right, and strode down the hallway towards his office. He dropped into his custom-made leather chair and pulled off his custom-made boots. At six foot eight and over two hundred fifty pounds, if he wanted anything to fit properly it had to be made especially for him. Fortunately, he had the money to afford it. But that hadn't always been the case.

Sinking into the comfort of the chair, he closed his eyes. He could feel the muscles in his shoulders relaxing. It was only then he became conscious of how tightly wound he'd been since he'd laid his eyes on her. A sigh escaped him and he realized, almost surprisingly, that he was tired.

His eye opened to a mere slit, but he could see it there in the corner. The only light in the room was focused on the painting that was propped on a wooden stand. He could feel the sensual pull of her form from here. He didn't even need to see it to be aware of it. Her image was burned into his brain.

There was an unselfconscious beauty about the woman in the picture. She was young, healthy and vibrant. Her hair was a study of brown and contained every shade from amber to almost blonde. She kept it cropped short, more for convenience, it seemed, than style. She was pictured in profile, but there was a hint of sky blue in the one eye you could see, and her flawless skin glowed in the golden morning light.

From the moment he'd seen the picture, Cain had wanted to possess this woman. He wanted to be the man who sat behind her on the stone steps. He wanted her to lean back into the shelter of his arms even as they shared the sunshine together. Cain wanted everything that the woman in the painting would give him. Her laughter, her companionship, her love.

He'd had to have the painting and had sent his trusted assistant, Martha Jones, to purchase it for him. Money was no object, but the owner had bargained hard. Cain could respect him for that. He'd also let it be known he was interested in other works by the artist, but so far he hadn't been contacted.

It had been sheer curiosity that had led him back to Coffee Breaks tonight. He'd wondered if he might find another painting in the window. Instead, he'd been taken aback by the appearance of the woman herself, come to life instead of just paint on canvas.

She was even more enthralling in real life. Not beautiful in the classic sense of the word, but there was something about her that called to the male animal in him. "*Mine!*" he'd wanted to shout to the world. Even in the dark of the night, there was lightness about her. She radiated warmth and light that was compelling to one who lived in the shadows.

His body had reacted immediately to her and, for the first time in a long while, he wanted a woman. She was now real to him and no longer just a dream. His erection had been both painful and reassuring. Hot on its heels had come an emotion he'd never felt before. Jealousy. Anger grew deep inside him at the knowledge that some artist knew her well enough to paint the very essence of her.

It had taken all of his control to remain hidden from her sight. But still, she had sensed him there in the dark. He'd sent Gabriel to her, to reassure her. Her laughter had been music to his ears and he had found a strange sort of contentment in just watching her walk home.

Disgusted with himself, he heaved himself out of the chair and deliberately turned off the light over the painting. Leaving the room shrouded in darkness, he padded down the hallway and into the master bedroom.

The room and the furniture were large to accommodate him. The bed was king-size, and the headboard and footboard were constructed of heavy oak slats. A pair of bedside tables flanked the bed which was covered in a forest green comforter. A huge oak armoire nestled against one wall while a matching chest of drawers rested against another. The large windows were normally covered with heavy green curtains in the daytime, but at night they were wide open so he could watch the night. His stocking feet sank into the plush green rug that sat in the center of the gleaming hardwood floor.

He stripped off his shirt as he walked through the bedroom and into the master bathroom. The only light came from a small night-light that rested just above the counter. Cain ignored it as he pulled off the rest of his clothes and tossed them in the hamper beside the tub.

Turning the shower on full force, he stepped beneath the pulsing spray. His body was alive for the first time in several years, and there was no relief in sight. He knew of several women who would be more than happy to fill his bed, as he had a reputation of being generous with his women. But that kind of arrangement no longer held any appeal for him. He wanted only her.

He lathered his body, mostly ignoring the ridges that covered his left arm and chest. After rinsing himself, he turned off the shower and used one of the large dark blue towels that hung on a heating rack to dry himself.

Wrapping the towel around his lean waist, he propped his hands on the counter and stared into the only mirror in the house. With his long damp hair slicked back from his face, there was no hiding from his frightening visage. The light was muted, but he could make out his features. "You're every woman's nightmare," he muttered to his reflection.

Turning slightly, the right side of his face appeared normal, not handsome, but not ugly. A twist in the other direction told a whole different story. His left eye was gone and his cheek still bore the scars from the fire. They continued down the left side of his neck to his chest and arm and stopped just above his leg. This was reality.

Stalking back to the bedroom, he dropped the towel over the bench seat that sat under the window and climbed into bed. Stacking his hands under his head, he contemplated the ceiling.

Every ounce of common sense was telling him to forget about her, but he knew that by this time tomorrow he would know everything there was to know about her. He drifted off to sleep with her still on his mind and his night was once again filled with erotic dreams where he indulged his every sexual whim. They were all of her.

Katie stared out the bedroom window at the street below. Most of the buildings were dark and traffic was practically nonexistent. The streetlights valiantly battled the darkness, waiting for the dawn. Nothing moved in the shadows. Not now, anyway.

There'd been someone there earlier. A man. She shivered at the thought. Should she tell Lucas? A woman who lived alone had to be careful, but Lucas worried enough about her as it was. Besides which, he'd had ample opportunity to hurt her this evening. Instead, he had sent his dog along to protect her.

But she wasn't totally naïve. This could be a ploy to win her trust. The news was filled with reports of sick people who did unspeakable things to unsuspecting women. Still, the dog was friendly, and that said a lot about the owner. Sighing, she turned away from the view and pulled the shade down so that most of the window was covered.

Knowing she wouldn't sleep, she decided she could at least work. Her bare feet made no sound as she padded down the short hall and into the small living room. Turning on the lights, she placed a blank canvas on the waiting easel. Her plain white nightshirt was worn thin and the light shone straight through it, highlighting the shape of her body beneath. Katie was unaware of this as she stared at the waiting sheet of white.

Her mood was strange tonight. It happened so rarely that she didn't recognize the sensation at first. She picked up a waiting brush and ran the soft bristles over her fingertips. She was lonely. Usually she was quite content in her own company and if she wanted to be with someone, she called Lucas for companionship.

How pathetic was that?

She'd worked her whole life. Part-time during school and full-time immediately after. Katie's grandmother had not been a young woman when her mother had left her here. But she'd never had any doubt that her grandmother loved her. They'd lived as simply as possible on her grandmother's pension and supplemented it with whatever work they could both find. It had been a godsend to them both when Lucas had hired her at fourteen to wash dishes. There'd been many nights that Lucas had sent "leftover" food home to her and her grandmother.

As a result, Katie had never had time to make close female friends. What few friends she had made had moved away to go to college and they'd lost touch. Since her grandmother died three years ago of a sudden heart attack, Katie had lived alone.

Well, almost. There'd been a brief six-month period where she'd had a live-in boyfriend. Kent. She rarely thought of him anymore. The only excuse she gave herself was that she was susceptible to his superficial good looks and charm so soon after her grandmother's death.

Kent had swept her off her feet with his boyish charm and classic good looks. With his windswept brown hair and his blue eyes, he was model perfect, and in fact had worked occasionally as a model. Very occasionally. Usually, he was content to stay home and live off her paycheck. She couldn't believe she'd let him sponge off her for six whole months. But with Kent, the big job was always just around the corner.

She really had Lucas to thank for opening her eyes. Lucas had walked her home late one evening from work. She hadn't even been through the front door when Kent had started yelling at her for not being home on time. He was furious that she hadn't been there to make his supper, and furthermore, he needed money to go out with his buddies. Didn't she know that they were waiting for him down at Frank's, his favorite sports bar?

Kent had reached out to grab her. Katie never knew if he'd intended to hit her or not. He never had a chance. One moment Kent was reaching for her, the next he found himself pinned against the living room wall.

In a low, menacing voice that Katie had never heard before, Lucas informed Kent that he was moving out. No, she laughed at the memory, what he'd really said was, "Get your stuff and get the fuck out."

Lucas had watched Kent's every move as he'd quickly collected his belongings. He might have been as tall as Lucas, but Lucas was massively built and Kent looked like a little boy next to him. Lucas's reputation had also preceded him.

Kent handed over his apartment key when Lucas demanded it, but couldn't resist a few parting comments as he hurried down the stairs. She could still hear him yelling, "You're nothing but a frigid bitch and I only stayed out of pity." She shivered as she remembered his parting words and wrapped her arms around herself to try and shake off the chill.

The look on Lucas's face had been the worst part. He looked so disappointed in her. Then he'd shaken his head and wrapped his arms around her and told her to cry. Surprisingly enough, she had done just that. After she'd cried herself out, he'd fed her soup and shooed her off to bed.

She'd awakened the next morning to the sound of an electric drill. When she'd peeked into the living room, Lucas was changing the lock on her front door. He calmly told her breakfast was in the oven and that was the end of it. Neither of them had ever mentioned Kent again.

No, she was better off alone. Work and art classes took up most of her time. Besides, she liked being able to get up in the middle of the night and paint. With that thought in mind, she turned her attention back to the waiting canvas. She saw the shadows forming in her mind and began to paint. For hours she stood there and mixed and painted. The picture in her head began to take solid shape in front of her. She painted until her fingers cramped and her back ached.

The first ray of sunshine hitting her face finally broke her concentration. The sun had obviously been up for a while. Groaning, she glanced at the clock on the VCR. "Omigod." Katie dumped the brush in a waiting jar. She was going to be late. It was already six-thirty and she had to open the shop at seven.

She hobbled down the hallway like a drunken sailor the morning after a binge. Her muscles ached all over her body and her head was spinning. She'd been painting for seven hours straight and she hadn't slept in over twenty-four hours.

Hauling off her nightshirt, she stepped into the shower, turning it on as she went. When the first splash of cold hit her naked body, she gave a yelp and quickly adjusted the water temperature. There was no time to enjoy her shower this morning. Lather flew as she soaped her body and her hair and then stood beneath the spray.

As soon as she was rinsed off, she turned off the taps and grabbed a towel. Her wet feet squished against the floor as she hurried to the bedroom.

Toweling off swiftly, she dropped the towel and pulled open her dresser drawer. Grabbing clean underwear, she tugged on her panties and then her bra. Socks, jeans and a long-sleeved blue cotton shirt followed. She snatched up the wet towel and hung it in the bathroom, while she paused long enough to throw her nightgown in the wicker hamper, brush her teeth and use the facilities.

Katie glanced at the clock as she grabbed her boots by the front door and tugged them on. Ten minutes since she'd first looked. She still had twenty minutes until the shop opened. If she hurried, she could get to work in ten minutes and get the coffee started before the regular customers started to arrive. She grabbed her faithful purple jacket, which hung on a hook by the front door, slung her purse over her shoulder and grabbed the keys out of her coat pocket. The white envelope crinkled in her pocket. "Damn it," she swore. She'd actually forgotten about the money. The bank would have to wait until later today as she had no time to stop this morning.

Out of habit, she glanced around the apartment to make sure she wasn't forgetting anything. As she scanned the room, her eyes hit the painting on the easel. She froze. As if tugged by some invisible string, her body edged towards the picture until she was standing right in front of it. It was only then that she realized what she'd painted.

The shadows and darkness of the night were illuminated with the faint light of the streetlamps. The figure of a man could be seen in the shadows. The man was huge and should have been menacing, but was somehow protective instead. The large, gray hound sat at his feet, waiting patiently for the man. Both man and dog were watching her from the darkness. Her hand reached out to touch him.

Katie yanked her hand away when she realized what she was doing. Reluctantly, she pulled her gaze away from the dark, compelling stranger. Another quick glance at the clock informed her that she'd wasted three minutes she didn't have to spare. "Katie, get moving," she muttered to herself as she hurried out the door. She twisted the doorknob twice to make sure it was locked behind her and hurried down the three flights of stairs to the street below. The painting was almost forgotten as she raced down the street. But it was there in the apartment. Waiting for her return.

Chapter Three

"You're the girl from the picture."

It wasn't a question, but a statement of fact. Katie smiled at the woman sitting at the small table by the window. A few people had recognized her from the painting that had hung in the window for several weeks, but not many. "Yes, I am." Katie placed a small menu in front of the woman.

"Do you know the artist?"

Katie looked more closely at the older lady. Definitely in her fifties, but she was more chic than grandmotherly. Definitely a businesswoman. Her hair was pure white, but it was styled in classic chignon. Her makeup understated. A cream-colored turtleneck sweater offset the rich plum of her suit. Discrete gold hoops adorned her ears. She was a picture of elegance.

"I know the artist," Katie answered. "Would you like something to drink, or would you like to order?"

The woman threw back her head and laughed. The unrestrained laughter made Katie smile in spite of herself.

"My dear, I appreciate a woman who plays her cards close to her chest, but you have nothing to fear from me." She was still chuckling when she reached into her slim, black leather bag, withdrew a vellum card with crisp black font, and handed it to Katie.

The card listed her name as Martha Jones and gave phone, fax, and e-mail address. The name was familiar, but she couldn't place it. "Do I know you?"

"We've never met, but I purchased the painting from Mr. Squires." She waited for a moment and then continued. "My employer is hoping to purchase more and would like to meet the artist."

"Miss. Can I get a café mocha to go?" The male voice startled Katie and she quickly glanced around. She was appalled to see the line up at the counter. "I'll be back in a few minutes." Katie scurried off before Ms. Jones could answer.

"I'll wait," Martha spoke softly as she settled back to watch the young woman work.

"I'm so sorry. What can I get you?" Katie's full attention was on the customer waiting first in line at the counter. For the next fifteen minutes, Katie filled all the orders cheerfully and competently. She'd caught Judy's eye and sent the young waitress to take Ms. Jones's order.

Katie was exhausted but she still summoned a smile as she bagged up two fudge brownies for a woman and her friend who'd just finished lunch. "Keep the change," the woman said as she handed Katie four one-dollar bills to pay for her two-fifty order.

"Thank you. Please come again." The response was automatic.

"We will. This place is great," the other woman replied as she took the bag of brownies and headed for the door. Her friend hurried after her, arguing good-naturedly that she would carry the cookies.

Katie pulled the tip jar from underneath the counter. It had been a good lunch crowd, and she and Judy would do well today. Lucas's policy was that whatever waitresses worked the shift split the tips. This was done daily and usually amounted to an extra five to thirty dollars a day each, depending on the crowd.

Shifting her weight to one side, Katie changed the money in the tip jar into bills and counted them into two piles. She managed a tired smile for Judy as she swung out of the kitchen with a tray of clean mugs and plates to be stored behind the counter. "Twelve bucks apiece. Not a bad day."

Judy tucked the money into her jeans pocket and tugged her crisp white apron with the store logo back into place. She gave her head a jerk towards the window making her short blonde ponytail bounce. "That woman is still waiting."

"I forgot all about her." She glanced at the table and Ms. Jones smiled back at her. Knowing she had no choice, Katie piled two strawberry tarts, utensils, a fresh mug and the pot of coffee onto a tray and headed over to the table.

"I haven't had breakfast or lunch today." Katie poured fresh coffee for Ms. Jones and placed one of the tarts in front of her. "These are the best, Ms. Jones," she added as she handed her a fork.

"Please, call me Martha. And by all means eat. After all, I'm interrupting your day."

Katie slid into the chair across from her and poured herself a cup of coffee. She took her time, added sugar and stirred slowly as she tried to gather her tired wits about her.

Scooping up a bite of the strawberry tart, she savored the taste as she chewed. She was aware of Judy in the background, clearing dishes and cleaning tables, but she was too tired to feel guilty. Taking a fortifying sip of coffee she addressed the mysterious Martha.

"What do you want to know about the artist?"

Martha dabbed at her mouth with the napkin. Katie noted that the strawberry tart was almost gone. Martha noted her gaze and laughed. "It's very good. I'm afraid I have a sweet tooth and couldn't resist." She leaned forward and stuck out her hand. "You know my name, but I'm afraid I don't know yours."

Katie was startled for a moment and then wiped her hand in her apron before shaking Martha's hand. "Katie Wallace."

"It's a pleasure to meet you, Katie. As I said, I recognized you from the painting immediately. It's a wonderful likeness of you."

"Thank you," Katie answered, as Martha seemed to be waiting for some response from her.

"You must know that artist well?"

"Yes."

Martha seemed impatient for the first time. "Is the identity of the artist such a big secret? My employer paid good money for that painting and is prepared to pay well if the artist has more that appeal to him."

"Then why doesn't your employer come himself?" Katie was surprised by her own audacity.

A reluctant smile crossed Martha's lips. "Touché, my dear."

Katie rubbed her hand across her forehead. The strains of the light pop music in the background only added to her already pounding headache. Usually, she enjoyed the radio, but after working all day on no sleep, it was more irritating than soothing. She was in no mood to banter with the stranger sitting across from her.

"Look, that painting was sold without the artist's consent or knowledge." Katie held up her hand to stop Martha from speaking.

"The artist won't make any trouble, but look at it this way. You have an artist who has never shown any work professionally, doesn't know if they're ready to do so yet, and suddenly has an anonymous man with lots of money interested in the work. In this day and age, it's not smart to give away too much information to someone you don't know. This wasn't a professionally brokered deal from a gallery." Katie took another sip of coffee to help steady herself. "If he wants to meet the artist he'll have to come here."

"That's impossible." Martha sat up straight, all signs of her smile gone. She was all business now.

"Why?" Katie was just as blunt.

"Mr. Benjamin rarely sees anyone."

"He'll see me if he wants to learn who the artist is." Katie rose from the table and piled the empty dishes and coffeepot back onto the tray. "Lunch is on me," Katie added as she picked up the tray. "I'm sorry you wasted your time."

"It was no waste at all." Martha stood and picked up her coat and purse. "I suspect we'll meet again."

Katie watched the older woman leave. Unable to stop herself, she yawned. She tightened her grip on the tray to keep from dropping it. Praying for some extra energy, she hauled the tray into the kitchen.

For the last year, Lucas had allowed her to work from seven in the morning until six closing, four days a week.

That gave her a full week's pay, but allowed her to have three days to paint or to take weekend art seminars. Since their customers were mainly from the surrounding business district, they were busier during the week than on Saturday. Lucas closed the shop on Sundays.

Today was Wednesday and she still had one day until the end of her workweek. Depositing her tray on the counter, she closed her eyes and allowed her fatigue to wash over her. She was no good to anyone feeling as she did. The lunch rush was over for today. It was time to go home. She made a mental note to stop at the bank on the way home and deposit the large wad of cash still sitting in her coat pocket. Lucas would let her go early just this once.

Katie stifled a yawn as she tugged on her coat, glad that it was finally Thursday evening. Lucas had left at three for a dentist's appointment, so she didn't have to deal with his scolding for working late. She'd felt guilty over leaving early yesterday, so she'd stuck around after closing and done some extra work.

Taking one last glance around the shop, she set the security lights and locked the door behind her, tugging on it twice to make sure it was secure. She'd left a note on the counter in the kitchen, letting Lucas know she'd cleaned the refrigerators and the ovens. Katie figured by the time she came back to work on Monday, he'd no longer be in the mood to scold her.

Hoisting her bag higher on her shoulder, she started for home. She pulled her purple leather gloves out of her pockets, and tugged them onto her hands. She loved the color, but never would have spent the money on something so impractical. Lucas had given them to her for Christmas, and wearing them always made her smile.

She took a deep breath. The night air was crisp and clear, but tainted by the unmistakable odors of the city. Underlying smells of exhaust fumes and garbage were still there, but the winter wind beat them back until they were only a hint in the air. It was much better than the stifling heat of the summer when the less-than-pleasant smells seemed to stick to every breath you took. It had been a long, strange week and Katie was actually looking forward to doing normal things this weekend, like laundry and housecleaning.

Mentally organizing her to-do-list in her head, Katie was absorbed in her thoughts and not paying her usual attention to her surroundings. Something struck her hand, jolting her out of her reverie.

Startled, she jumped back and swung hard. She spun around, meeting nothing but air. Taking a quick survey of her surroundings, she noticed the dog from the night before sitting calmly in front of her looking bemused at her paranoid actions.

Katie's heart was pounding in her chest, but her relief was so great that she started to laugh. Her laughter had a hysterical edge to it that she was unable to suppress. The dog casually licked his front paw and glanced at her as if to ask her what was so funny.

Leaning down she confronted her new friend. "You scared me," she admonished even as she reached out her hand to scratch the dog under the chin.

"We didn't mean to scare you." The voice was low and deep and came from the shadows to the right of the building. "We hope you'll accept our apology." Katie backed towards the streetlight and glanced around for help.

"You wanted to meet me," he added quickly. "My name is Cain Benjamin."

Katie racked her brain, trying to remember why that name was familiar. Just as she made the connection a low, rough laugh came from the waiting man. "Obviously, I overestimated your eagerness to meet me."

Katie felt herself blush, flustered by his sudden appearance. Not wanting to appear rude, she stuck out her hand. "Please to meet you. I'm Katie Wallace."

The man in the shadows hesitated. Katie waited until the moment stretched past what was socially acceptable. Feeling awkward, she dropped her hand back to her side and stuffed it in her pocket. The dog beside her started to whine and shuffle back and forth from her to the man in the shadow as if sensing their agitation.

A deep sigh came from the shadows. "I'm not pleasant to look at, Ms. Wallace." As he spoke, he moved from the shelter of the building.

Katie looked up. Way up. She stood frozen to the spot by the sheer size of him. He was dressed normally enough in boots, jeans and a leather jacket, but there was nothing else normal about him. She'd never seen a man as tall or as massively built as the one standing in front of her. The collar was turned up on his coat and his long black hair hung over the left side of his face, partially shielding it from view. A black patch covered his left eye, its thin strap bisecting his forehead before disappearing into his hair.

He moved forwardly slowly as if trying not to scare her. She assured herself that any sane woman would be terrified of this tall stranger. Yet, for some unknown reason, she was not. What that said about her, she didn't want to speculate. Her usual common sense had disappeared, replaced with a growing fascination about the man in front of her.

He came to a stop a few paces from her, allowing her space. Not crowding her. She appreciated that small kindness. This was a man who knew he was intimidating and was trying his best to make her comfortable with his presence. She could have told him that he was wasting his time.

Katie didn't think anyone could ever be comfortable in this man's company. He radiated such a powerful magnetism that attracted her even as it warned that this was a man who would not be controlled. His right eye, the one she could see, was pale green and had a steady patient look in it.

Gathering her courage, Katie swallowed the lump in her throat and stuck out her hand once again. "It's good to meet you, Mr. Benjamin."

His large hand closed carefully around hers. It disappeared for a moment, engulfed by the sheer size of his. He held her hand so long that she began to get nervous and tugged on his grip. Her hand was immediately released. "Call me Cain. It's a pleasure to meet you, Katie. Martha told me that I'd like you."

The wolfhound bumped impatiently against Cain and then sat in front of Katie. "And you've already met Gabriel."

"You followed me home the other night." Katie glared at Cain. "You had no right to scare me like that."

Cain stuck his hands in his jacket pockets, but the move made him only slightly less threatening. "I didn't mean to follow you. I was walking by Coffee Breaks to see if there was another painting in the window. Instead, I saw you." He gave a small self-deprecating laugh. "I will admit that I bought the painting as much for the subject as the artist's skill. You're beautiful."

Katie was speechless. She'd never thought of herself as beautiful before. That someone would spend that much money on a picture because she was the subject was mind-boggling. And scary.

As if reading her mind, he continued to speak. "I'm not a stalker, Katie. Just a man who appreciates beauty in all forms. I would never harm you."

Strangely enough, Katie believed him, despite every instinct she had developed after years of city living. The steady look in his eye and the way he held himself away from her told her that she had nothing to fear from him.

She noticed the way that he kept his right side towards her and his left side angled away as if it was his natural way of standing. The left side of his face was in shadows so she studied the other side, which was the epitome of strength. His cheekbone was high and his square chin looked like it was chiseled from stone. His lips were full and his eyebrow a slash of black against his pale complexion.

"Not very pretty, is it?"

Katie flushed in shame as she realized that she'd been standing there just staring at him, but answered him honestly. "No, pretty is too weak a word. Your face is strong."

He looked taken aback by her blunt comment and then the corner of his mouth quirked up in an amused smile. "Now you sound like a parent trying to comfort a small child. I can assure you that it's not necessary."

Katie instinctually knew that for some unknown reason, her opinion was very important to Cain. Hoping she was doing the right thing she gave him the truth. "No, I sound like an artist." She held her hand out to him once again. "I'm Katie Wallace. I'm glad you like my self-portrait."

Once again his hand clasped hers. This time he drew her into the shadows and then faced her fully. "I was jealous of the artist."

Katie stared hard, trying to discern the left side of his face, but with no success. "Why?" she asked as she continued to blatantly stare.

"Because he had obviously spent time with you. Because he knew you, and I wanted to."

"Are you always this blunt?" Katie was taken aback by his reply. She took a step backwards, towards the light, but Cain retained possession of her hand. It seemed silly to fight him, so she stopped tugging on her hand, stood her ground, and glared at him.

"Always," he replied. He grinned, looking almost boyish for a moment, and tucked her hand in the crook of his arm. "Would you walk with Gabriel and me? We'll take good care of you and make sure you get home safe." When she hesitated, he quickly added, "We were on our way to the park to play. I only take him out at night. It's quiet there and we can talk."

Despite her better judgment, Katie answered the only way that she could. "Yes."

He tucked her closer to his side and matched his longer stride to hers as they strolled through the dark streets towards the park. The night air was cold, but Katie was warm and cozy as Cain's large body sheltered hers.

Cars sped by, sirens wailed, and occasionally the sounds of raised voices filled the air. But the sound was almost muted, muffled somehow by Cain's very presence.

Chapter Four

Cain's large body radiated heat, which enveloped Katie as they walked together. She instinctively snuggled closer to him, drawn to the warmth and comfort he provided. It was completely out of character for her to be so rash. Yet, strolling arm in arm with this virtual stranger, Katie was surprisingly content.

Neither of them spoke as they meandered down the almost deserted sidewalks. The silence was comfortable, rather than awkward. Cain steered them unerringly through the dark shadows of the buildings and away from the streetlights. The action seemed as natural to him as breathing.

Why was she here? Katie glanced quickly to her left, but she could only see the right side of his face and very little of that. Her eyes went back to the dark pavement in front of her as she contemplated the enigmatic man beside her. Yes, she found him handsome in an interesting sort of way, but it was more than that. There was something about him that attracted her on a far deeper level. *But what?*

Katie bit her lip as she mulled these questions over in her mind. Butterflies fluttered in her stomach. But underlying her nervous reaction was a feeling of anticipation. It was the same feeling she'd had when she'd first picked up a paintbrush. Her life was about to change in some unalterable way.

"Watch your step." Cain's voice was a whisper in her ear. His lips grazed the edge of her ear as he spoke. A shiver ran down her spine, but she ignored it as he guided her up a set of unlit stairs. The sound of their footsteps echoed through the dark. His large hand on the small of her back protected her from stumbling backwards. "Just a little further."

The sound of his voice reached deep inside her, stirring to life feelings she didn't recognize. What was it about this stranger that enticed her? That tempted her to do such a foolish thing as walk with him on a dark, deserted street? It wasn't his looks, as she had only glimpsed one side of his face. Yet there was something in the way his entire energy focused on her when she spoke. His green eye was like some wild beast's, sharp and intense, as he watched her. He made her feel fascinating and interesting.

He was naturally protective of her as they walked, tucking her arm securely in his and automatically using his sheer size to keep the cold winter wind from assaulting her. There was a strength, both physically and mentally, about him that was mesmerizing. A sureness when he walked. A sense of purpose.

The feeling of grass under her boots tugged Katie from her musings. Glancing around, she realized that they had entered a small park. There were some well-lit paths, but they were well away from those, sheltered in darkness by the large trees. "It's very hard to see where I'm going." Her voice trembled slightly. A fine time to get nervous, she scolded herself.

"You'll get used to it." He gave a sharp whistle as he strode onto the field and Gabriel came bounding up to him. As she watched, he removed a length of rope from his pocket and threw it. Gabriel raced off in pursuit, a large blur of gray that was eventually swallowed up by the dark.

"Get used to it," she muttered crossly. "Why would I want to get used to it?"

Katie jumped when a pair of strong arms enveloped her from behind. Like a ghost, he moved so quickly and silently that she hadn't noticed him sliding behind her until his arms wrapped her in their strength. Her mouth and throat both went dry and she tried to swallow her rising fear. He was a stranger to her, and she had willingly put herself in his power.

"The night is a place of beauty, Katie." One of his large hands coaxed her closer to him until her back was pressed tight against his chest. She could feel the solid muscle of him through their coats. Her breathing was shallow and quick, creating a slight fog in the air in front of her.

While one of his hands anchored her to him, the other one moved up over her chest, pausing for a moment to stroke her breast before coming to rest at the side of her head. She was taken off-guard by his boldness but said nothing, waiting anxiously to see what he would do next.

He nudged her face against his shoulder and then cupped her chin, turning her face upward slightly to meet his gaze. "Let me show you."

Katie held her breath as he lowered his face towards her. The rational side of her was screaming to break away from this man, but the emotional part of her desperately wanted to know his kiss. His touch.

Slowly, his lips grazed hers. Barely touching. He moved away and stared at her. Waiting. "Let me show you," he repeated. His rough fingertips gently traced the curve of her cheek. He was a sorcerer, and she was helpless to resist the dark spell he was weaving around them.

Katie tipped her head towards him ever so slightly. It was all the consent he needed. His head lowered once again. Katie's stomach fluttered with anticipation as she waited for him to kiss her. Some previously unknown part of her yearned for his kisses. Instead he teased her with light touches of his lips. He kissed her lips, her cheeks, her nose.

"Close your eyes." He was like a solid rock behind her, waiting for her to follow his directions. For a moment, her common sense rose to the fore, demanding to know what in the hell she was doing. But Katie ignored it, and closed her eyes, enjoying the softness of his lips as he dropped kisses on her eyelids.

"Keep them closed and embrace the dark," Cain instructed in a whisper as his lips skimmed hers. His teeth grasped her lower lip and he nibbled on its fullness. Katie moaned and tried to deepen the kiss, but he pulled away.

Katie's eyes opened and she stared up at him. "Why?"

He hushed her and rocked her in his embrace. "Close your eyes and let me give to you. Take what I offer you." She could feel him waiting patiently for her to decide.

His sheer sized dwarfed her, and the arm he had wrapped around her was like a solid band of steel. She knew she could not escape him unless he released her. The very idea scared her even as she found herself aroused by the realization that she was at his mercy.

Katie's uncertainty grew, but the lure of his kisses was too great to deny. As she closed her eyes, she caught a glimpse of satisfied triumph in his face, and then the darkness was complete. She was rewarded when his lips once again sampled their way down her face to her lips.

His grip on her waist tightened, as if he were afraid she would change her mind. This time his lips seized hers in a long, deep kiss. His tongue forged its way into her mouth and claimed it. He dueled with her tongue before capturing it and sucking on it. Wielded his tongue like a rapier, he advanced and retreated until he had won her completely. Her legs weakened, but he held her easily in place and she let herself go, trusting him to keep her upright.

The world no longer existed. Sheltered in the dark of the trees, away from the footpaths and the lights, the night was a secluded and seductive haven. Vague sounds of traffic and the barking of a dog were nothing but dim background noise, drowned out by the pounding of her heart. For Katie, there was only Cain.

Her feet left the ground as Cain lifted her easily and moved them both deeper into the surrounding trees. Startled, Katie opened her eyes as her feet touched the ground again. Cain turned her body so that her back was against a tree, and he stood in front of her. The two of them were completely isolated from the rest of the world, as the only sounds were their breathing and the wind whistling through the tree branches.

"Trust me," came his sorcerer's voice from the darkness.

Cain undid the front of her coat and slipped it down off her shoulders. She shivered as the cold night air sank through the thin layers of her clothing. His hands grasped hers and raised them over her head, wrapping them around a low tree branch. She could feel the rough texture of its bark through the thin leather of her gloves.

"Hold on tight. Don't let go." Obeying his instructions, she gripped the branch tightly, her fingers slightly chilled beneath their thin covering. It was her only support. She could hardly believe she was doing this.

The coolness of his hands was startling as he unbuttoned her top to reveal her bare stomach and her bra. His fingers skimmed over her stomach, causing the muscles to contract. He laughed softly as his fingers reached for the front closure of her plain cotton bra. His nimble fingers made quick work of the fastener, and he pushed the cups aside. Her nipples puckered in the cold night air. Katie shivered. She felt exposed. Vulnerable. Sexy.

Taking his time, he positioned her so that her back was tight against the tree, and her hands were anchored firmly to the overhead branch. Stepping back, he looked at her for a moment before pressing both elbows back. This time when he looked at her, he nodded in satisfaction. "Beautiful. Now don't move."

Katie could feel the wetness between her legs and was almost embarrassed by it. Never had she played these kinds of games with a lover before and she was shocked by how turned on she was by his commanding presence. With her arms extended and her elbows wide apart, her breasts were thrust forward as she waited for him to touch her.

The heat of his mouth was shocking as he took one tight peak in his mouth and sucked. Hard. Katie moaned and pushed closer to his lips. Cain cupped both breasts in his large hands, holding them captive as he continued to pleasure her. His clever fingers tantalized and pleased one breast even as he used his talented mouth on the other.

"So damned beautiful," he muttered as he went from one breast to the other. Tasting. Teasing. He captured one nipple between his teeth and nipped it carefully.

Katie was alive with sensation. It was if every nerve ending in her body was connected to her breasts. Her entire body was alive and screaming for more. Unable to help herself, Katie dropped her hands to his shoulders and tried to tug him closer.

As soon as her hands touched him, he grasped them and returned them to the branch. "If you want me to pleasure you then you have to keep your hands where I put them."

Katie swallowed nervously. "I can't," she whispered. Averting her gaze, she scuffed the toe of her boot across the frosty ground.

Cain sighed deeply and used a finger to tip her chin up to meet his heated gaze. He placed a tender kiss on her lips, as his hand cupped her jaw more firmly. "I can help you if you'll let me."

"What do you mean?" Katie's uncertainty grew as he reached into his coat pocket and drew out what looked like a leather dog leash.

"I rarely need it, but it does have other uses." He stepped away from her and held the leather strap in front of him.

Katie's hands automatically covered her breasts as she tried to back away from him only to find herself against the tree. Cain nodded and started to replace the leash in his pocket. "I'll take you home."

His voice was calm and accepting which gave Katie the courage to ask, "What would you do with it?" She couldn't believe she hadn't run through the park screaming, but she was hot and restless with what they'd already done, and part of her, she had to admit, was curious.

"I'd never hurt you," he promised. "This is just a tool to help you keep your hands where I put them." The leather leash was pulled tight between his huge hands. "If I tie them to the branch then you don't have to worry about moving them. All you have to do is relax and allow me to pleasure you as I choose."

His voice whispered through the night, seducing her with his words. The thought of being totally at his mercy, captive to his every whim frightened her even as it aroused her. She could feel her nipples growing harder against her crossed arms. Her legs were weak, and she could feel her wet pussy clenching, aching to have him inside her.

He stepped closer to her, his booted feet crunching on the ground. When he was directly in front of her, he raised his hands and let the leash dangle between them. "It's your choice. If you refuse, I'll take you home. You can pretend it never happened, and I won't bother you further."

Katie instinctively knew that if she refused him she'd never see him again, and she didn't want that to happen. This virtual stranger had aroused her passions more than any other man ever had. But was she willing to take the chance?

"Choose." His voice was tinged with irritation now as if he was losing patience.

Afraid that he might change his mind and leave, she raised her arms in front of her before slowly clasping her hands together and offering them to him. Cain's expression never changed as he carefully wrapped the leather strap around her wrists, and then raised them high above her and tied the leash around the tree branch.

Katie felt a momentary panic as she tried to move her hands and could not. Unable to help herself, she struggled for a moment before Cain stopped her. "There's no need to hurt yourself." His voice soothed her and she subsided. When she was calm once again, his hands pushed the edges of her top open again until she was full exposed.

Taking his time, he ran his hands all over her torso and back. She arched towards him, wanting him to touch her breasts again, but tied up as she was, she was unable to make him do anything. Her frustration grew even as her skin heated up. Cain nuzzled her breasts, tasting them before finally flicking the nipples with his tongue. The relief was so great she almost came on the spot.

"Yes," she moaned. "More," she encouraged. Her entire body swayed in an erotic dance.

It was a new experience for Katie to allow a man to control her passion, and much to her surprise, she found that it heightened her own arousal. It made her even hotter that he had exposed her body in a public place and was now playing with her. Controlling her by promising her even more. She never wanted him to stop. The heat he created inside of her kept the cold night air at bay. Katie had never felt this wanton in her entire life. It scared her. But, it excited her.

Cain seemed to sense the change in her, and he wrapped her firmly in his embrace. There was no way for her to escape him now even if she was so inclined. And she wasn't. His attention to her breasts never wavered, but his hand quickly flicked open the button on her jeans. The zipper quickly followed and then his hand slid beneath her panties.

Katie spread her legs, giving him total access to her. Encouraging him wordlessly to touch her clitoris, to stroke her with his large, thick fingers. She rocked her hips towards him while her hands clenched desperately on the tree branch. "Touch me," she cried.

He pushed her jeans and panties down to her knees and groaned when his hand was met with the wetness and heat of her desire. One of his fingers slid deep inside her and she could feel her muscles closing tightly over his finger. Katie moaned and moved against his finger, unable to stop herself, not even sure she wanted to stop. Cain slid a second finger in to join the first. Stretching her. Bringing her closer to orgasm. Katie could no longer think at all. Her entire being was focused on the pleasure he was bringing her. Her fingers dug deep into the tree, trying to keep herself grounded.

"No, don't stop," Katie pleaded when his mouth left her breast. But Cain ignored her as he kissed a hot trail up the side of her neck. The tip of his tongue traced the whirls of her ear before dipping inside it. Katie was caught in the web of Cain's dark seduction. His breath was coming faster now and his body was tense. It was enthralling to be the focus of all this barely leashed masculine power.

His voice was barely a whisper as he licked the tip of her ear once more before nibbling the line of her jaw. Katie arched her head to give him better access. "Come for me," Cain commanded before his lips covered hers in a searing kiss. His tongue moved in a rhythm that matched his fingers. In and out. Deep and steady. On and on he played her body in the velvet of the night.

Forgotten was the fact that they were in a public park, and that she was virtually naked, exposed to the night. The world narrowed to the two of them. Katie could feel the muscles of her body tightening, reaching for completion. Nothing else matter, not even her next breath. Her entire focus was on Cain and what he was doing to her body.

Katie sucked his tongue hard as she felt the force of her orgasm wash over her in waves. Her mind went blank as she gave herself over to the power of the pleasure. Her legs buckled, but Cain ruthlessly held her up and kept moving his fingers. She could barely breathe as his mouth continued to devour hers. Her climax went on and on. The cool air on her hot, damp skin added to the intensity of her orgasm. She shuddered and rubbed her clitoris against his thumb one more time, wanting to milk the experience to the very last drop.

Cain gently removed his fingers from inside her. She shuddered at the loss. Peppering her face in kisses, he murmured indistinguishable words of praise and encouragement as he reached up and untied the leash.

Gathering her in his arms, he sat on the cold ground, unwound the leather from around her wrists, and cradled her in his arms. One large hand swept up to push a wayward lock of hair off her forehead. She could smell herself on his fingers, and shivered as a flicker of arousal sprang to life inside her again. Katie hadn't thought it was possible to be aroused again so quickly as she'd never felt more replete and relaxed in her entire life. In truth, she hadn't known her body was capable of such an amazing and powerful climax.

As she sunk into his arms, she could feel the hardness of his erection pressing into her side. Suddenly, she was very aware of her vulnerable state. Her clothes were half off, in a public park, and she was in the embrace of a very aroused, extremely huge, stranger. She shivered, suddenly aware of the cold as the sexual heat of the moments before began to fade.

She'd never done anything this uninhibited or irresponsible in her entire life. Her body felt lethargic, but she was almost lightheaded with the power of her emotional and sexual release. Thinking was beyond her.

Cain's fingertips soothed her swollen lips and she was instantly aroused again. "Taste yourself, Katie." He rubbed his finger along her lips until they parted enough for him to skim the inside of her mouth.

Unable to resist his lure, she licked at his finger, tasting the essence of her sexual release on him, breathing in the musky scent of sex and desire. She felt like some strange erotic creature and not like Katie Wallace at all. The muscles in his arms tightened in response, so she sucked hard on his finger, wanting to savor the moment. Her tongue licked his finger clean.

Cain slowly withdrew his finger and shuddered as she scraped her teeth across his skin. "What am I to do with you, Katie?"

"What do you want to do with me?" The question was out of her mouth before she had the wisdom to stop it. Her voice was husky and full of erotic promise. She didn't sound like herself at all, but rather like a wanton seductress.

"Everything," he replied starkly, his voice a husky whisper. "But, for now, I'll just take you home." He stood with her still cradled in his arms, as if she weighed nothing. Holding her tight, he held her close for a moment before he reluctantly released her legs and allowed her to stand on her own.

Clutching his arm for a moment, she regained her balance and stepped away from him. She felt cold and bereft without his touch. The reality of it suddenly sank in. She'd just played kinky sex games in a public place with a man she'd just met.

Awkwardness fell over her as she struggled to fasten her bra, button her shirt, and tug up her jeans. She could hear the dog barking in the distance and the muted sounds of the never-ending city traffic. Now that the moment was past and her common sense was reasserting itself, she felt clumsy and totally inept. She didn't even bother trying to tuck her shirt back into her jeans. It was enough for her to be covered from his gaze.

Cain found her coat and plucked it from the damp ground. He shook it hard and then held it for her as she slipped into it. She was grateful for its warmth as her body was now racked with shivers, equal parts cold and nerves.

Cain cursed in the darkness as he buttoned her coat and tucked her under his arm. "I'm sorry you're cold." He rubbed his hands briskly over her arms and back until the shivers gradually subsided. Tucked in his arms, she could feel the heat returning to her body. Leaning down, he kissed the top of her head before releasing her.

Her eyes were glued to the leather leash as she watched him roll it up and return it to his pocket. She shivered, and this time it wasn't with the cold. What could he have done with her?

Neither of them spoke as he guided her back onto the path. The warmth of his hand at her back seemed to burn through the layers of her coat and shirt. Cain gave a sharp whistle and Gabriel came running from the other end of the park, rope toy dangling from his mouth.

Katie was well aware that Cain was still fiercely aroused as he walked her towards home. The rather large bulge in the front of his jeans was a dead giveaway, and the arm wrapped around her shoulder was as solid and hard as a piece of steel. His jaw was clenched tight, and his stride was stiff.

Now that the moment was over, she was appalled at her own recklessness. She was no tease, but neither was she ready to sleep with Cain. She'd already given him more of herself than she had to any other man, and that included Kent.

"Cain, I don't do things like that," she began, only to stop when he gave a hoarse laugh.

"I didn't think you did." His voice was edgy and tight.

She stared at him in the darkness, unable to make out his mood. "I didn't mean to be a tease..." she trailed off uncertainly.

Cain was instantly alert beside her. He stopped and turned so his right side faced her. "You're not a tease. You gave me a gift this evening." He paused to gather his thoughts. "I want more. I want to spend time with you. I want you in my life. In my bed."

His raw statements were almost as frightening as they were arousing. She'd never been the focus of this much male attention before in her life. "Who are you?" Her life was spinning out of control and she didn't like the feeling.

"I'm just a man. Nothing more."

Katie glanced away, seeking relief from the intensity of Cain's gaze. Relief washed over her as she noted her familiar surroundings. She'd been so wrapped up in her inner turmoil that she'd paid absolutely no attention to where they were walking. Subconsciously, she had trusted Cain to take her home. Still, her pace quickened as they rounded the corner and her building came into view. Cain said nothing, but adjusted his pace to hers.

She wanted to be home where she felt safe. This stranger had knocked down all her defenses, and she felt vulnerable. He had touched her artistic soul when he bought her painting, and he had touched her physically and emotionally with his lovemaking. She knew nothing about him. Nothing at all.

Katie ducked from under Cain's arm, raced across the street, and up the lighted steps of her apartment building. She needed to get away from him. To get her equilibrium back. Her thoughts were scattered and her emotions were raw. She could feel him watching her desperate escape from the shadows.

"Good night," she called, pulling her keys from her pocket as she mounted the stairs.

"Katie, don't be afraid." His voice carried clearly on the night air. She didn't want to look. Told herself she wouldn't look. But when he called her name again, she was unable to resist the lure of his voice. "Just spend some time with me. We'll wait until you're sure, because there's no going back." She could feel the heat of his stare even from this distance.

Katie didn't even try to formulate an answer. Jamming her key into the lock, she turned it and charged through the door, slamming it shut behind her. She fled up the stairs, not stopping until she gained the safety of her apartment. He'd made no move to follow her, but still she felt compelled to run. Her breathing was ragged, and tears stung her eyes.

Whether she was running from him or from herself, she wasn't quite sure. All she knew was that her life had changed. She was not the same woman who left this apartment this morning. Cain had tapped into a wanton side of her that she hadn't known existed. The lure of sexual pleasure was great, and for the first time in her life she wasn't sure she could resist its call.

Chapter Five

Katie scrubbed the bathroom with a vengeance. The white porcelain of the bathtub gleamed and the chrome taps sparkled in the morning sun. She'd tossed and turned all night long, unable to get Cain out of her mind. The sun was just rising when she dragged herself out of bed, determined to put him out of her mind and get some work done. It was now just before noon and the small apartment had been swept, scrubbed, and dusted from top to bottom.

Katie sat back on her heels and surveyed the bathroom. She peeled off her rubber gloves and swiped her hand over the sweat on her forehead. Images from the night before flashed through her mind. She still found it hard to reconcile the woman from the night before with the woman she normally was. She'd been reckless and somewhat stupid in venturing off with an unknown man. And what she had done with him! Just thinking about it made her feel hot and tight all over, as if her skin no longer fit her properly.

Rising from the floor, she picked up her bucket of dirty water and dumped it down the toilet. Giving the handle a quick downward push, she watched as the dirty water swirled around for a few seconds and then disappeared, leaving cleaner, fresher water in its place. She wished her own thoughts could be discarded as easily. Sighing deeply, she picked up her rubber gloves and sponge and dragged it all to the kitchen closet where she stored her cleaning supplies. The fresh smell of lemon cleaner and the bright glow of winter sunlight filled the air. Her apartment was clean and tidy, but she was a mess.

Katie stared out her small living room window. For once, she was not noticing the sights and sounds of the neighborhood that usually enchanted her. Street vendors enticing people to their carts with the savory smell of food, children playing on the sidewalk, the colorful display of the newsstand on the corner, and the varied groups of people rushing down the street. This was usually a source of unending inspiration for her painting. She was only vaguely aware of it, as a sort of hazy vision off in the distance, but she couldn't seem to focus her attention on any of it today.

More often than not, she found the mundane housekeeping tasks almost restful. There was something soothing about the repetitive chores of sweeping and cleaning that allowed her mind to drift into a state of almost artistic meditation. Unfortunately, this morning it hadn't worked.

Katie felt restless. She was startled to realize that she was waiting, but wasn't sure what for. Cain had left her uncertain last night. *Would he contact her?* She didn't know how to reach him even if she wanted to. The real question was *did she want him to?* Closing her eyes, she tilted her head back and allowed the fatigue to wash over her. She didn't know what she wanted, but she had an unsettled feeling in the pit of her stomach that she had to find out where this thing with Cain was leading. If she didn't explore it, she'd regret it for the rest of her life.

She rolled her head from side to side to loosen the tension in her neck. One thing was for sure, she was finished moping. It was a beautiful winter day, crisp and clear, and she had things to do. First, she would take a shower and then she'd take herself to lunch at Gino's Italian Deli before she went grocery shopping. Thoughts of spicy Italian food started her mouth watering and her stomach growling.

The painting on the easel caught her attention as soon as she opened her eyes. It was no longer complete, but rather was the beginning of what she feared would be a series of works. The dark shadow from this painting now had substance. Cain was real to her now and no longer a night phantom.

Her emotions always found their way onto the blank canvas and already her brain was picturing and discarding many possibilities. Idly, Katie picked up a dry brush and tapped it against her chin as she was drawn into the painting. She needed to see more of him this time. Removing the finished canvas, she propped it next to the wall where she had a clear view of it. She grabbed a fresh, blank canvas and positioned it on the easel.

A loud knock on the door made Katie scowl. She hated to be interrupted when she was working. It was probably just as well, she thought as she lay the brush down. She really needed groceries. Katie opened the door, but kept the chain on as she peeked through the opening.

"Delivery." A young man in a delivery uniform tapped his foot impatiently as he waited for her to respond.

"But I didn't order anything," Katie answered suspiciously. In all the years she had lived here, she had never had a delivery of any kind. "Are you sure you have the right apartment?" It had to be a mistake of some kind.

The young man glanced at his clipboard. "You Katie Wallace?"

Katie nodded hesitantly.

"Then it's for you." He laid the box on the floor when she still made no move to open the door. "Look, I just need a signature here." He thrust the clipboard through the small opening. "The tip has been taken care of. Just sign on line three."

Katie scribbled her name on the proper line and pushed the clipboard back towards the deliveryman. Glancing down to make sure his paperwork was in order, he turned and hurried away. "Have a nice day," he muttered as he disappeared down the stairs.

Katie waited until his steps faded and then she cautiously unlocked the door and picked up the large white box. Propping it against her hip, she relocked the door and then carried the package to the coffee table. Carefully, she removed the cover and peeled back the crisp, white tissue paper. She forgot to breathe as she peered down into the box.

Her fingers tentatively reached out to touch the flowers, tempted by their lush, burgundy petals. The box overflowed with long-stemmed roses. There had to be at least two dozen of them and their heady scent filled her nostrils as she took a deep breath. The blood-red roses were a sharp contrast to the one perfect orchid that lay in the center of the box. Its white petals and pale pink center looked all the more fragile surrounded by the roses. It was a gift of sensual promise. Of passion.

A white envelope was tucked into the tissue paper and Katie plucked it out. She didn't need to open it to know who had sent them. Still, she was curious enough that she opened the envelope and drew out the plain white card. The writing was bold with a masculine bent, making her think that he'd written the message himself. "I'll call you at midnight," she read aloud. Nothing else. Not even a signature.

Katie placed the card carefully on the coffee table. She couldn't decide if the message was more threat or promise. The gift was an extravagant one. Katie didn't even want to contemplate the cost of the exotic flowers. They were hers and she planned to enjoy them. Grabbing up the box, she hugged it and laughed out loud. She danced her way into the kitchen, her feet shuffling as she swung her hips from side to side. Setting the flowers carefully on the counter, she rummaged around the cupboards for a container to put them in.

Settling on two Mason jars for the roses, she carefully positioned the flowers one at a time in the containers until she was satisfied with their placement. The thorns had been removed and that made the task much easier. She floated the orchid in a Depression glass bowl that she'd found at a thrift store. The pale pink of the glass matched the center of the exotic bloom.

Katie stood back and admired the flowers, enjoying the rich texture and color, and slightly drunk on the heady perfume of the roses. She hugged herself in glee, feeling like a kid on Christmas morning. One at a time, she moved the containers into the living room and placed them in various positions until she found one she was satisfied with. One jar of roses sat on the windowsill, their beauty framed in the morning sun. The other one sat in solitary splendor on the coffee table and the orchid bowl perched alongside her easel so she could admire it while she worked.

Her stomach growled, reminding her that she'd promised herself a spicy Italian lunch. Katie glanced at her watch and was surprised to see that almost an hour had passed. It was almost one o'clock.

Reluctantly, she headed for the bathroom. She had to shower, change, and then head out to run her errands. Katie couldn't resist one last glance behind her as she left the room. The sight of the flowers filled her stomach with butterflies and a feeling of anticipation.

Katie stepped back from the easel and contemplated her latest work. Tipping her head to one side, she examined it from another angle. It was better than good. She'd managed to capture the sheer animal magnetism of the man, his image half-hidden in the shadows while the half illuminated by the streetlamp showed a man of power. A sense of danger and darkness surrounded him, as if he were a predator just waiting to pounce. This was a man who valued control and exerted the power of his will on those around them. She'd had a firsthand lesson in that last night.

Cain's was not a handsome face, but a strong and a surprisingly sensual one. His hair blended in with the black of the night and fell over the left side of his face. His nose was large and had a bump in the middle, but it suited his face well. His jaw was square and his cheekbones were prominent. But it was his eye that drew her. She'd managed to capture the intensity in his startling green eye.

Her back ached and her fingers cramped as she stood there. Katie groaned and stretched, but her eyes never left her painting. She'd been working for hours. When she'd left the apartment at lunchtime, Katie had planned on a leisurely lunch before running her errands. Instead, she'd grabbed a quick pepperoni and salami sandwich, raced through the grocery store, and hurried home to work. The need to paint Cain was almost overwhelming. Her fingers were itching to paint and she readily succumbed to the temptation.

Satisfied for the moment, Katie cleaned up her brushes and set her supplies to rights. The empty feeling in the pit of her stomach informed her that she had missed supper. She shrugged, unconcerned. It wasn't the first meal she'd missed. When she was painting, time seemed to disappear as she immersed herself in her work.

The kitchen beckoned and Katie answered the call. She quickly washed her hands and assembled a quick snack of cheese, crackers and slices of crisp green apple. Stopping long enough to grab a bottle of water from the refrigerator, she carried her booty to the living room.

Sinking into the comfort of the well-worn sofa, she munched on an apple slice as she tilted her head back and closed her eyes. She was tired, but it was good kind of tired. A satisfied kind of tired. She was pleased with her latest effort. One eye popped opened and glanced at the clock. Just after eleven. And she was pleased that she had managed to keep her mind off Cain's mysterious message.

She shook her head and sat forward. Who was she trying to kid? Cain had filled her thoughts all day. It didn't matter if she was cleaning, shopping, or painting, her mind continually turned to him. Piling a cracker with cheese, she stuffed it into her mouth and chewed. It would serve him right if she went to bed and turned off her phone.

But she knew she wouldn't.

When her plate was empty, Katie took it to the kitchen and dumped it in the sink. Taking her time, she checked to make sure the lock was on the front door, turned off all the lights and went into the bedroom.

The light from the bedside table was soft and muted as Katie undressed for bed. She made a quick trip to the bathroom to attend to her nightly rituals of washing her face and brushing her teeth. The sheets were soft and inviting as she crawled under them, taking a moment first to adjust the comforter on top.

Katie settled her head against her pillow and stared at the ceiling. Squirming around, she tried to find a comfortable position. She lay there for a moment before flinging back the covers and thumping down the hallway and into the darkness of the living room.

It took her two trips, but the three containers of flowers now graced her room. One jar of roses sat on the bedside table while the other one graced the windowsill. The orchid bowl was centered in the middle of her dresser, reflected in the mirror behind it.

Katie snuggled back into bed again and took a deep breath. The scent of roses filled the air, and she sighed in contentment. She inhaled deeply again. Then once more. The worries and thoughts of the day started to melt away and she felt herself relaxing for the first time all day.

She drifted in that state of wakefulness and half-sleep until the shrill ring of the telephone shattered her tranquility. Her body immediately reacted. Her heart pounded and her hand shook as she reached out to answer the call. It was one minute after twelve.

"Hello."

"Did I wake you?" Cain's voice was deep and husky on the other end of the line.

"No. I'm in bed, but I wasn't asleep." Katie tucked the cordless phone under her ear. She could hear nothing but the sound of Cain breathing on the other end. "Are you there?"

"Yeah," came his reply. "I'm picturing you in bed. Are you naked?"

"No. No I'm not," Katie stuttered in reply. "I have on a nightgown." Katie could feel a heated blush climb up her face. "What are you doing?" She desperately wanted to change the subject.

"I'm sitting in the dark in my study." Cain gave a short, harsh laugh. "I've been sitting here for an hour, waiting to call you."

"Thank you for the flowers." Katie felt shy all of a sudden, as if Cain could somehow see her. She burrowed under the covers, pulling them tight to her chin and grasping their soft edge with one hand.

"You're very welcome, honey." Cain's voice flowed over her like a warm blanket and made her feel very special.

Silence filled the other end, and Katie fidgeted with the covers while she waited for him to continue. She didn't know what to say to him, but she was strangely content to just listen to the sound of his breath and his voice. Her contentment was shattered with his next request.

"Take off your nightgown, Katie," his husky voice pleaded.

"Why?" Katie wasn't sure she liked his tendency to want to dominate their sexual relationship.

"I want to imagine you naked in your bed. Waiting for me." His bold words shocked her even as she felt her body responding to them. She clamped her legs together and squirmed a little to try and ease the ache.

"Why do you always want to be in control?" Maybe this wasn't the best time for such a question, but she genuinely wanted to know his answer. At first, she thought he might ignore her question. Fidgeting with the bedcovers, she waited impatiently.

"It's as natural to me as breathing. You liked it last night didn't you, Katie?" His tone was soft and coaxing. "I certainly did."

"I did enjoy it." She could feel the heat of a blush cover her face. "I'm not completely at ease with that fact, and I don't know that I want it to be that way all the time." Unable to find a comfortable position, she turned on her side, and plumped the pillow under her head.

"I see." He paused for effect. "Do you want me to go?"

"No." Her heart was pounding now and she could feel a bead of sweat drift down her back. Part of her was afraid that he'd just hang up, and part of her wished he would. "I just don't want to be ordered around all the time."

"Will you do what I ask tonight?" His sorcerer's voice was urging her to agree.

When she made no reply, he tried again. "There's no harm, Katie," he coaxed her. "You can do it."

Squeezing her eyes tight, she counted to five and made her decision. There was no way she could resist the soft plea she heard in his voice. "All right." She hardly recognized her own voice as she heard herself agreeing.

"Wait," Cain called. "Can you put me on speakerphone?"

Katie looked at her machine. She'd never done it before, but she knew her phone had the capability. "Wait a second." Katie pushed a button and stuck the receiver on the phone base. "Okay."

"Can you hear me all right?" Cain asked. His deep voice seemed to fill the room.

"Yes."

"Then strip for me, Katie." His request was stark.

The rustling of bedcovers could be heard in the silence. Anticipation filled her as Katie pulled her nightgown over her head and let it fall by the side of the bed. She took a deep breath and tugged the covers back over her. Her breasts nudged the underside of the cool sheet, and it was arousing to feel her torso and her behind sink into the sheet that covered the mattress. "I'm naked."

"Push the covers down, Katie." The rustling covers had given her away. "Lie back on the bed like you were waiting to entice me." Cain's voice was ragged as he spoke.

Could she do it?

His quiet "Please" filled the air. Katie bit her lip, uncertain. Making up her mind, she kicked the covers off the bed so they wouldn't tempt her. "I'm naked on the bed for you." She couldn't believe that sexy voice was hers.

"What do you look like?"

Katie looked at her body, and saw only her familiar, lanky form. She looked away as she spoke. "I look like me." Cain's husky laugh filled the other end.

"Tell me everything," he ordered. "Start at your toes and work your way up."

Katie swallowed and stared at her toes. "My feet are big."

Cain's laughter echoed through the bedroom. "They're not as big as mine are, honey. I wear a size fifteen."

Katie continued, feeling a little more confident now. "My legs are really long, but they're strong from all the walking I do."

"Someday soon, I want to feel those long, luscious legs wrapped around my waist. You'll hook your ankles tight around my back as I bury my cock deep inside you." Cain's voice sounded strained as he spoke. "You'll like it. I promise."

Katie bit her lip to hold back a moan as his words created a very vivid picture in her mind. She could imagine them, legs entwined, with Cain thrusting deep and hard inside her. Her skin heated, and she could feel the dampness between her legs as her body prepared itself to accept him. That was the problem with being an artist, she could visualize the entire act. Perfectly. Well, maybe it wasn't such a problem after all.

His voice called out to her. "Katie, tell me more."

Katie moved her legs restlessly on the bed, as the throbbing ache between her legs grew stronger. "My hips aren't too wide, but my waist dips in a little." Her hands traced the curve of her hip and grazed the side of her waist. She'd never touched herself in a sexual way before. The thrill of doing something slightly illicit was potent.

Cain responded as if he could read her mind. "Is your skin warm? Are your nipples hard?" His voice got lower and softer. "Are you wet for me?"

Katie was half-scandalized and half-turned on by Cain's questions. "Yes," was all she could manage to say. She felt all those things.

"Tell me," he ordered.

Katie licked her lips. She could feel her nipples getting harder. "My nipples are hard."

"What color are they?"

"Dusty rose."

"Touch them for me," he groaned.

Katie's hands slid up to cover her breasts. Their fullness filled her hands. Her nipples grew even tighter as she massaged them and plucked at them with her fingers. She moaned and her legs came together to try and ease the throbbing emptiness. She wanted release.

"Are you touching yourself?"

"Yes," she moaned. "I ache."

"Do you have the roses nearby?" Cain questioned.

"Yes," Katie replied as she turned her head to admire them.

"Take one of them in your hand." Cain waited while she followed his instructions. "Now close your eyes and pretend the petals are my fingertips. Draw the petals over your legs and up your stomach."

Katie clenched her teeth and let out a low hiss as she did as he asked. The soft petals against her sensitive skin aroused her unbearably. "Let the petals slide over your nipples. Back and forth. Back and forth." His low voice was hypnotic, and she blindly followed his instructions.

Katie got lost in a world of sensual pleasure as she drew the rose over her nipples. The slight friction of the petals on her nipples was driving her crazy. Their velvety softness caressed her breasts and teased their hard tips. It was too much and not enough at the same time. She needed more. She needed Cain, but he wasn't here.

The scent of the flower was intoxicating, as her breathing grew more rapid and uneven. Katie was caught in the sensual snare of Cain's voice and no longer hesitated at his commands.

"Put a pillow under your ass and spread your legs for me, Katie." Katie grabbed the pillow next to her and stuffed it under her behind, and then she spread her legs without a moment's thought. "Wider." Cain ordered. Cain paused for a moment. "Are you open wide for me, Katie?"

"Oh, yes," she moaned, straining to open her legs wider. "Only for you."

"Keep them open as wide as you can."

"Yes," she promised, pushing them even further apart.

"Put your middle finger in your mouth and suck on it. Hard." His odd command jolted her for a moment, but she complied and began to lick and suck her finger. "That's good," he praised her. "Now, spread yourself wide with your other hand and use your wet finger to lightly rub your clit."

Katie moaned as she did as he'd asked. Her heels dug into the mattress as her hips pushed upwards. The air was thick with the smell of her arousal mixed with the pungent scent of the roses as deep moans slipped from her. She was so close to coming, and her entire being was focused on her pleasure.

"Keep your legs open. That's it. Just keep your touch light and steady." Cain's breath was deep and harsh as it filled the room. "Now, slide that finger right up inside your wet pussy. Feel your muscles clench around it." Katie pushed her finger deep inside and arched up as her inner muscles clench it. She could hear Cain talking in the background, but could barely understand what he was saying. A second finger joined the first one deep inside her.

"God, I want my cock deep inside you. It would feel so damn good." Katie could hear the pain and longing in his voice. "Pretend that your fingers are mine. Use them however you want. However you need. I want to hear you come."

Katie continued to move her fingers, finding a rhythm that pleased her. Using her thumb, she brushed her clitoris and moaned in pleasure. Cain's voice kept up a steady stream of encouragement and praise. "Reach for it, baby."

Katie's breath was coming harder and faster, but it still wasn't enough. "Cain, help me..."

"Pinch one of your nipples hard, Katie, but don't stop moving your fingers. You're so close, baby."

Katie was sweating now. She could feel the perspiration roll down her forehead. Without thought, she followed Cain's instructions. Rolling one of her taut nipples between her thumb and forefinger, she then pinched it. At the same time, she thrust her fingers as deep inside her as they would go. "Your fingers are longer," she wailed.

"I wish I was there. I'd eat your sweet pussy until you came. Imagine it, Katie. Imagine me doing that for you. Because I will, you know. I'll lick your clit and suck your lips until you cry for mercy, but I won't stop. Not until you come in my face. Soon, Katie," he promised. "Soon."

Katie was moaning and thrashing on the bed. So close. She was teetering right on the edge.

"Come for me, Katie. Come for me. Now." At Cain's final command, she brushed her thumb across her clitoris and rode the wave of sensation.

Desire reached a feverish pitch and Katie reached for it. Her orgasm washed over her, filling her completely before releasing her. She fell back in bed, exhausted and replete, but strangely empty at the same time. Her legs moved restlessly over the sheets even as her body thrummed with pleasure. She wanted Cain here with her. In her.

"You're beautiful in your passion, Katie." Cain's voice was deep and rough in her ear. "Next time, I want my cock to be in you when you come. I want you to want that, Katie."

His words were making her feel hot and bothered all over again. The hand on her breast began to move again, stroking her engorged nipple. "Yes, Cain." She felt so good right now. "I want to feel you inside me." She shivered as the hand between her legs began to stroke her wet, aching flesh.

His strained laughter filled the other end. "You sure make it hard on a man."

Katie suddenly became aware of the fact that she was sprawled wantonly on her bed having phone sex with Cain. She closed her eyes and groaned even as she reached over the end of the bed and pulled the covers up over her naked, sensitive skin. "I'm sorry."

"Why? You just gave me a beautiful thing. Thank you." As if he could hear her thoughts he went on. "Don't feel awkward or guilty. We both enjoyed ourselves."

"All right," Katie promised, not sure she would be able to keep it. "I won't."

"I'll see you soon, Katie. Sleep well and dream of me."

She could hear him breathing on the other end of the phone and knew he was waiting for her to sever their connection. "Good night, Cain. Sleep well." She heard him muttering to himself as she reached out and broke the connection.

Smiling to herself and hugging his "not likely" to her heart, Katie turned off the bedside lamp and settled into bed. She reached under the covers and pulled out the slightly squashed rose and placed it gently on the pillow next to her head. Her body reacted to the intoxicating scent of rose and sex that filled the air. Katie's movements were slow and sensual as she settled her bare skin against the sheets. She didn't bother with her nightgown. Being naked made her feel closer to Cain. She drifted off to sleep with a smile on her face and his promise in her heart.

Chapter Six

The rest of the weekend dragged on for Katie. All day Saturday, she waited for him to call. It had been a beautiful day, but she'd stayed inside like some lovesick teenager waiting for the phone to ring. Several times, she'd picked up the receiver and checked for a dial tone. Everything was fine, but the phone still didn't ring.

She went to bed Saturday night anticipating another late-night call. Nothing. She lay awake half the night, furious with both Cain and herself. Him for not calling and herself for caring.

Sunday, she ran out early in the morning for a quick run to her favorite bakery a few blocks over. Usually, she enjoyed her leisurely Sunday morning breakfast out. She'd linger over her coffee and pastry and do some sketches of the street or whatever people interested her. But that day, she'd rushed home instead and waited for a call that never came. By evening, she was livid with herself for wasting her weekend waiting for him. Dreaming about him.

The thought of what she'd done on Friday night made her face burn. Phone sex. Her. Yet Cain had made it seem not only exciting, but also totally natural. Katie had to admit, if only to herself, that she never would have done it without Cain's suggestions and encouragement. The thing that surprised her most was how much she'd liked it. For the first time in her life, she felt a sexual freedom that she'd never experienced. She'd done more things out of character since she'd met him than she'd ever done in her entire life.

By the time Monday morning arrived, she was glad to go to work. She obviously needed a dose of reality to get over her miserable weekend. After tossing and turning all night long, she'd decided she might as well go to work and be productive. When she arrived early for work on Monday morning, the lights were already on in the kitchen.

Katie let herself in through the front door, taking care to lock it behind her. She tucked her gloves in her coat pocket and dumped her purse on the countertop. Sliding behind the front counter, she started four different kinds of coffee. Even though it was only a few minutes after six, from the delicious smells filling the air, Lucas had been hard at work for quite some time.

Katie slung her purse back over her shoulder and pushed her way in through the kitchen door, striving for her normal cheerfulness. "Good morning." She breezed by Lucas, planting a kiss on his cheek as she passed him on her way to the office.

Pulling open the office door, she slipped inside, breathed a sigh of relief, and began to remove her coat and boots. She'd passed the first test. There was no way she wanted Lucas to notice she wasn't her usual self. He'd ask questions until he got answers. And right now, she didn't have any answers to give him.

It was only when she was tying the laces on her white tennis shoes that it occurred to her that Lucas hadn't spoken. In her own desperate bid for normalcy she had failed to notice that all was not right with him. Giving her laces a final tug, she stood and pulled a clean "Coffee Break" apron on over her long-sleeved white shirt.

Satisfied that she was ready for the day, she strolled back to the kitchen and watched Lucas out of the corner of her eye.

Outwardly, everything seemed fine. He looked the same as he always did. Big, solid and steady. His face was a study in concentration as he worked. There seemed to be nothing physically wrong until she noticed the set of his shoulders. Tense. That was the only word to describe him. He lacked the fluidness of movement he usually possessed in the kitchen. Normally, watching Lucas bake was like watching a beautifully choreographed dance, sometimes fast, sometimes slow, but always a joy to behold. This morning he looked about a step behind.

Taking her time, she readied the staff coffeepot in the kitchen and set it to brew. All the while she kept her eye on Lucas. He continued to pour ingredients into a bowl, stopping to stir or measure occasionally. The scrape of the spoon on the side of the metal mixing bowl and the water dripping from the coffeemaker were the only sounds. Katie said nothing as she waited for the coffee to brew and filled two mugs when it was ready.

Carrying both mugs, she plunked one down in front of Lucas. "You seem like you could use this." She climbed onto the stool next to him and waited.

"Yeah, thanks." Reaching forward, he snagged the mug and took a large swallow before he finally looked at her. His eyes were bloodshot and the lines around his eyes seemed more pronounced.

"What's wrong?" Unable to restrain herself any longer, she went to him, wrapped her arms around his waist, and just held him. At first he held himself stiff, but when she showed no signs of letting go, he finally sighed and his arms drew her closer.

His heart thumped steadily beneath her ear. He inhaled deeply and then exhaled slowly, relaxing as he did. Lucas just stood there for a moment, breathing deeply and holding her securely in his arms. Finally, he gave her one final squeeze and pulled away. Reluctantly, she released him.

He rubbed a hand across his tired eyes before reaching into his apron pocket and pulling out a folded sheet of white paper. "Read it." He tossed it on the counter in front of her and crossed to the oven to check on pans of cookies he had baking inside.

She lifted the seemingly innocent piece of paper, unfolded it and began to read. Paying no attention to the sender, she went right to the heart of the letter and read the entire thing. Then she read it again. And again. Finally, her eyes went to the top of the letter to the corporate logo, but the company, E. S. Investors, meant nothing to her.

Lucas removed four steaming pans of cookies from the oven and placed them on a rack to cool. The smell of chocolate chips, oatmeal, and coconut seemed to mock her instead of offering their usual comfort.

"This..." she trailed off and began again. "This can't be right. They can't kick you out of this building. You don't rent from them."

Lucas tensed for a moment and then turned back to the cookie trays. Using a large metal spatula, he scooped the cookies from the pan. Methodically and carefully, he moved them a few at a time. "Apparently, they can. This E. S. Investors has bought the building and not only ours. There's quite a few businesses in the next two buildings as well who are going to have to relocate."

"But you have a lease." Katie was in shock. Coffee Breaks had been in this spot since it opened almost fifteen years ago.

"And it's set to expire in a few months. I've always signed a five-year lease." Lucas piled some cookies on a plate and carried them to the counter. The early morning sun was starting to peek in through the small kitchen window, making the kitchen a warm and cozy spot. The two of them had spent many such mornings together, sipping coffee and sampling cookies.

Pulling up another stool, he sat next to her and took another sip of his coffee. "I was expecting a lease renewal, not this."

"Can't we fight it?" Katie could feel anger begin to override her sorrow and fear. That some nameless, faceless corporation could turn her life upside down was just too much for her to take.

"It's all perfectly legal." Lucas reached out and plucked a warm cookie from the plate. Taking a bite, he chewed thoughtfully as steam rose from the uneaten half still clutched in his hand. "Actually, it's good of them to let the leases expire rather than evicting everyone. I did some research over the weekend, and this company is rich enough to buy out the leases if they wanted to and close everyone down tomorrow. At least I've got some time to find a new space."

Katie stared at Lucas in amazement. "How can you be so calm about this? This is your life."

His fist slammed down hard on the counter, making her jump. "What do you expect me to do, Katie?" He didn't yell, and the very softness of his voice was more frightening.

Taking a deep breath, he gained control before facing her again. "I'm sorry, honey. I didn't mean to frighten you."

"Oh, Lucas." She held her hand out to him and waited until he took it. "You don't scare me. This does." She poked the offending letter with her index finger. "It will change everything."

"Maybe it's a blessing in disguise." Lucas moved away from her and pulled out another clean bowl from the cupboard. Placing it on the counter, he then began assembling ingredients. It was all done automatically. Lucas had a phenomenal memory and rarely used a recipe anymore.

"How can you even think that, let alone say it?"

"It's not the first time my life has changed unexpectedly." Lucas poured sugar into the bowl, continuing to work as he talked.

Katie watched him as he calmly measured flour and dumped it into a sifter. "I guess not."

"Besides, it's not like I'm going to close the place. I'm just going to relocate it and, in fact, this time I want to try and find a building I can afford to buy so this doesn't happen again." He carefully sifted the flour into the bowl and then thoroughly mixed it with the sugar.

Katie was amazed at his resiliency. "You've been thinking about this?"

"For a while now." Stopping for a moment, he wiped his hands on a towel and came back over to sit beside her. "When I first opened, I could barely afford to rent the place." He laughed. "Buying a building was nothing but a dream. But now I've got some money saved and a good business record. I'm thinking about something not too big but with other spaces or apartments I could rent out."

He reached out and tapped her on the nose. "Maybe I'll find a place with a couple of apartments and I'll live in one and rent you the other. Or maybe you'll become a famous painter and this will get you moving on in your career." Bending down, he brushed a kiss on her forehead. "This could be a good thing for both of us."

Katie couldn't stop the tear from rolling down her cheek any more than she could stop her next breath. "But I don't want things to change."

"Things always change. It's how you handle it that counts." He glanced up at the clock. "Enough of this for now." Using the corner of his apron, he wiped the tear from her face. "We open in fifteen minutes and we've both got work to do."

Katie slipped off the stool and left Lucas to his baking. Like a sleepwalker, she walked behind the counter and efficiently moved the full pots of coffee to the warmers and set more coffee to brewing. She hurried back and forth to the kitchen, carrying trays filled with fresh baked treats back out front and setting them in the glass case. Quickly, she counted out the store money and readied the cash register for the day. It was a routine that she'd had for many years and she didn't think about it, she just did it.

At exactly seven, she unlocked the door, removed the closed sign, and greeted her first customers of the day. The smile on her face might have been forced, but her customers never noticed. Fate was kind in giving her little time to brood as the day got busy quickly and didn't let up until closing.

That evening, when the apartment door closed behind her, Katie was more than ready to lock the world out. She leaned against the door and tilted her head back. Closing her eyes, she tried to ignore the headache forming ominously behind her eyes. It had been an impossibly long day.

Lucas had taken her out for pizza after they'd closed the shop for the night. She'd managed to consume one slice of pizza and munch the pepperoni and peppers off another slice. But she'd been too upset to really eat. Usually, she easily held her own with Lucas when they pigged out on pizza. Lucas, on the other hand, seemed to experience no such problem. He'd quickly polished off the rest of the fully loaded supreme pizza all by himself.

Ironically, he had spent all his time reassuring her that everything would work out for the best when it should have been the other way around. She hadn't realized how much she depended on the stability of the coffee shop until it was threatened. What if the new location was far away from her apartment? Or worse, what if Lucas couldn't find another location before the lease was up? Would she be unemployed? She shuddered at the thought. She'd never been unemployed a day in her life.

Pushing away from the door, she dropped her bag on the floor and removed her coat and boots. "I need a hot bath and chocolate," she muttered to herself. A tub filled with bubbles and hot water while she sipped real cocoa from her favorite mug. That was the best medicine for her burgeoning headache.

In the kitchen, she filled the kettle with water and set it on the stove to boil. While she waited, she pulled down a big pottery mug done in a cheerful yellow and placed it on the counter next to the milk, sugar, and cocoa powder.

Rummaging around in the cupboard, she found a round tin with a few chocolate-dipped shortbread cookies in it. She pulled one out and munched while she waited for the water to boil.

Two cookies later, her mug was filled with hot chocolate and she was ambling down the hall towards the bathroom with the tin of cookies stuffed under her arm. The shrill ring of the phone broke the silence. She really didn't want to talk to anyone. When the phone rang for the fourth time, she gave up and went back to the living room to answer it. If it was Lucas and she didn't answer, he'd be pounding on her front door within fifteen minutes.

Juggling her mug and the tin of cookies, she grabbed the phone on the fifth ring. "Hello." There was a moment of silence on the other end. "Hello," she said again, her voice sharp.

"I missed walking you home tonight."

Katie sucked in a breath, her heart pounding at the low seductive voice on the other end of the line. Then her common sense reasserted itself. "I wasn't expecting you. We didn't have plans." Her reply was cutting as she'd spent all weekend waiting for him to call her.

"No, we didn't have plans, but I still missed you." He paused and when he spoke again his voice was rough. "I didn't like seeing you leave with Squires."

"You were watching me and Lucas?" Outrage filled her. "Lucas is more than just my boss and my friend. He's all the family I have, and I'll spend as much time with him as I want. I have a life and what I do is my business." There, that ought to put him in his place. She got nervous as the silence on the other end grew. While she wanted to assert her independence, she didn't want him to walk away from their budding relationship. With all the changes in her life, she didn't know if she was coming or going, but she knew she wanted to spend more time with Cain.

A deep sigh filled the line. "I know, but I still didn't like it. I want your life to be my business. I want to be part of your life."

It was said so reluctantly that Katie took pity on him. "We just went out to supper to discuss some business matters." She perched on the back of the sofa and took a quick sip of hot chocolate. The pounding in her head was getting worse.

"So, it was business, nothing personal." He sounded relieved by her admission.

"It sure feels personal," she muttered.

"Business is never personal." Having made that pronouncement, he deftly changed the subject. "I'm sorry I didn't call yesterday but I got tied up with some business. I'd like to make it up to you if you're willing."

"What did you have in mind?"

"Have dinner with me tomorrow night. I have to go out of town for a few days after that, but I want to see you before I go."

Katie was itching to ask where he was going and what he did for a living, but she hadn't quite worked up the nerve to do so. Something about him was so closed and reserved. Chewing on her bottom lip, she considered his invitation. It might give them a chance to really talk to one another. This could be her chance to learn more about him.

"It's just dinner, honey," his voice, laced with humor, filled her ears. She hadn't realized she'd been quiet for so long.

Drawing on all the courage she possessed, she made her decision. Deep down, she knew her acceptance would suggest agreement to more than a simple dinner. She was making a commitment to at least explore this connection between them. "All right, I'll have dinner tomorrow night."

"I'll send a car for you after work."

"No, I want to come home and change first." There was no way she was going out to dinner in jeans and a shirt she'd worked in all day. "How about half past seven?"

"Your wish is my command." She could tell by the tone of his voice that he was humoring her, but she didn't mind.

"I like the sound of that," she teased.

"Tomorrow, Katie. Sleep well." The other end of the line went dead, but Katie wasn't concerned. In many ways, his abrupt manner reminded her of Lucas.

Hanging up the phone, she gathered her warm chocolate and cookies, and strolled down the hallway to the bathroom. She would need to figure out what to wear tomorrow night. Something casual, yet pretty.

Taking a sip of her drink, she then laid it on the side of the tub for easy access. After a moment's hesitation, she placed the open tin of cookies next to her mug. Turning on the taps to the tub, she pondered her choices while she ran hot water and added bubbles. When the tub was full, she stripped off her clothes, and dumped them in the hamper.

Slowly, she eased into the tub, sliding beneath the mound of fragrant lavender bubbles. She took a face cloth and dumped it in the water before slapping it over her forehead. The heat felt good against her throbbing forehead. Reaching out her hand, she patted the side of the tub until she reached her mug. Carefully, she lifted it and took a sip before returning it to its original position. Taking a deep breath, Katie slid down further in the tub and contemplated her unexpected dinner date.

Chapter Seven

Squeezing a glob of shampoo into her hand, Katie quickly lathered her hair and stuck her head under the showerhead. Sputtering a little as soap ran into her eyes, she valiantly ignored it and squirted some body wash into her sponge and began to scrub her body. When soapsuds covered her from head to toe, she ducked back under the showerhead and allowed the hot water to wash away the dirt and grime of the day.

Why did she have to be late getting off work today of all days? It was if the fates had conspired to keep her rushing around all day. For the first time ever, her alarm clock hadn't gone off and she was late for work. And she hated being late. It seemed that no matter how hard she tried she never quite caught up.

Then a regular customer had called late in the afternoon, pleading with Lucas for several dessert trays for an emergency meeting at work. What could she do? She could not desert Lucas. Laughing at her own choice of words, she jumped from the shower, grabbed a towel and started drying herself.

Katie couldn't remember the last time she'd had anything resembling a real date. She was more excited than she'd thought she'd be. Wiping the steam from the mirror, she peered at her reflection. There wasn't much to be done with her hair so she just ran her brush through it. Her cheeks were flushed from the shower, but she looked pale.

She chewed on her lower lip for a moment before coming to a decision. Rummaging under the bathroom sink produced the little yellow zippered pouch she was looking for. Taking a deep breath, she pulled back the zipper and peered inside. Makeup. She loathed the stuff, but had worn quite a bit of it while dating Kent. He'd encouraged her to wear it, to play up her assets.

Poking around inside the bag, she produced a tube of mascara and a tube of pale lipstick. While opening the mascara she prayed that it wasn't completely dried up and was rewarded when the wand came up with stuff on it. Squinting, she applied mascara to her lashes. When she was finished, she grabbed the tube of lipstick and slicked some over her lips. Surveying her reflection in the mirror was not an encouraging sight. She looked like she was wearing bad false eyelashes they were so clumped together and come to think of it, the lipstick wasn't quite the same shade it used to be.

Giving up in disgust, she grabbed a face cloth, ran it under some warm water and scrubbed at her face until the mess was gone. It took longer than she'd hoped as, rather than coming straight off, the mascara made nice little gray rings around her eyes. She wasted another five minutes just getting herself back to the state she'd been in when she'd gotten out of the shower. Sighing, she wrapped herself in a towel and hurried into the bedroom.

Grabbing a bottle of unscented lotion from her dresser, she slathered some on her body. As she rubbed her legs, she thanked the dating gods that she had shaved them last night. There was no way she would have had time to do it tonight. She tugged on a pair of stretchy lace underwear and a matching bra. She really didn't need a bra, but it was the principle of the thing. It was a set, so she would wear both pieces.

"Oh, no." A quick glance at the clock showed her that it was exactly half past seven. A knock came on her front door. She stood frozen for a moment, staring at the clothes that she had picked out last night. Nothing looked right for tonight. Another knock echoed up the hallway. This one more insistent.

Grabbing her robe from the hook behind the door, she tugged it on as she hurried down the hall. Making sure it was belted tight, she pulled open the door and then promptly slammed it again. Putting the chain on the door, she opened it a crack.

"Can I help you?" Katie knew that her actions were erratic, but that was exactly how she felt right now. Who the heck was this guy? She didn't have time to deal with whoever this was. Cain would be here any minute.

The stranger covered his shock at her strange behavior, drew himself upright and replied in a dignified manner. "The car is here for Ms. Wallace."

Katie looked at him suspiciously. "What car?"

The uniformed man, who looked to be in his late fifties, took off his hat and tucked it under his arm. He raised his head for a moment and Katie couldn't be sure if he was asking for divine intervention or was studying the cracks in the ceiling. She thought it was the former. She took the moment to check him out. He was few inches taller than her and built like a bulldog with short graying hair and a nose like a beak. The artist in her noticed that his eyes were almost the exact same shade as his gray hair.

His eyes twinkled with humor as he looked back at her. "Mr. Benjamin has sent a car for you. Please feel free to call him and confirm." He rattled off a phone number that she assumed was Cain's.

"Just a second." She closed the door in the man's startled face for the second time in under a minute and hurried to the phone. Dialing the number the stranger had given her, she tapped her foot and waited as it rang three times before it was abruptly answered.

"Benjamin."

Katie was taken aback by the harshness of his answer and it took her a moment to find her own voice. Cain lost patience with the silence and snapped again. "Who is this?"

"Katie."

"Why aren't you here?" She could hear the impatience in his voice and her own temper snapped.

"I'm running late and I've got some strange guy at my door saying he's here to pick me up and I'm not ready yet." She stopped when she realized not only was her voice getting shriller, but she was rambling. Rubbing her fingers across her forehead, she hoped that this wasn't going to become the date from hell. It was certainly starting out that way.

There was silence on the other end for a moment before the sound of Cain's booming laughter filled the line. She'd never heard him laugh in quite this uninhibited way before and she had a feeling that it was something he didn't do very often. Even though it was at her expense, she found she didn't mind at all. Just listening to his unrestrained laughter made her smile.

"I'm sorry, honey." He coughed and sputtered as he obviously did his best to get his wayward humor under control. "I thought I was the only one panicking over this evening. It's nice to know otherwise."

She was both mystified and charmed by his answer. He seemed so self-assured all the time and so curiosity prompted her to ask, "What do you have to worry about?"

"The better question might be what don't I have to worry about? What if you don't like dinner? What if you don't enjoy yourself? What if this evening makes you never want to see me again?" There was laughter in his voice as he answered her and although Katie thought he was only teasing her, it was nice of him to put her at ease. Because that was what his banter had done.

Feeling more relaxed than she had all day, she brought his attention back to her original question. "Cain, who is the guy at my door?"

"That's Quentin. I use his services sometimes and I sent him to pick you up. Listen, you take your time and get ready. I'll call him on his cell and tell him to wait for you." His voice was husky and made her shiver as he continued. "Take as long as you need. We've got all night."

That very thought gave her goose bumps, and her voice was shaky when she replied. "All right."

"See you when you get here." The line went dead and she hung up the receiver. A second later she heard the faint ringing of a phone in her hallway and heard a male voice respond.

Unable to stop herself, she padded back to the door and removed the chain before opening the door again. He was startled to say the least and eyed her warily as he finished his conversation with Cain. She waited until he was finished and then stuck out her hand. "Hi, I'm Katie Wallace. Pleased to meet you."

He stared at her hand for a moment before his bemused eyes met hers. Slowly, he took her hand in hers and gently shook it. "James Quentin at your service."

Katie smiled at him and motioned him inside. "You might as well come in and sit down while I finish getting ready."

He dropped her hand and stepped back. "Ah, no thank you, miss. Mr. Benjamin would not approve."

"Who cares? This is my home and I say please come in out of the hallway. I'll never get ready if we stand here arguing about it." When he still hesitated, she reached out and grabbed him by the uniform sleeve and tugged. Reluctantly, he allowed himself to be pulled inside.

"Have a seat, I'll just be a couple of minutes." As she headed back down the hall, she turned and called over her shoulder, "And call me Katie."

Closing her bedroom door, she flung off her bathrobe and tugged on the brown wool pants she'd laid out last night. Her favorite silk shirt in a beautiful shade of oatmeal followed. She topped the outfit with a long-sleeved beige cardigan made of raw silk that she'd picked up at the thrift store for a song. The outfit not only made her look good, it made her feel good.

She sat on the bed and tugged on a pair of brown leather boots. They had little zippers on the sides and were more for fashion than for function, but for five bucks at the thrift store she had been unable to resist. She lovingly referred to them as her "kick-ass" boots because when she wore them she felt as if she could take on the world.

Slipping a small pair of silver hoops in her ears, she surveyed her appearance. Turning first one way and then another she smiled in spite of herself. "Not bad, girl. Not bad at all." She gave her reflection a wink before she snatched up her purse and left the room.

Quentin was standing in the corner of the living room. His attention was fixed on the painting on the easel. He turned when he heard her and gazed at her with something in his eyes that looked like respect. "You've captured him perfectly."

"Thank you. Do you really think so?" Katie hated feeling unsure about her work, but Cain was such a hard subject.

Quentin nodded slowly. "Yes. Yes, I do."

Feeling a little uncomfortable, she grabbed her coat and tugged it on. Quentin hurried across the room, but she had her coat on by the time he reached her. "Shall we go?" He opened the door and held it for her. Katie stopped long enough to lock the door behind her and then Quentin led her to the car waiting below.

Cain was pacing impatiently when he finally heard the mechanical hum of the elevator rising. Everything was ready, and now that she was finally here his evening of seduction could begin. If everything went according to plan, and he had no reason to think that it wouldn't, then Katie would not be leaving here this evening.

The last few days had been hellish for him, and he needed her. He wanted to lose himself and his problems in her body. All night in bed with Katie was just the therapy he needed.

The elevator finally came to a halt and the door slid open. Katie stepped out, looking more beautiful than ever, but a frown covered his face when he realized she wasn't alone. Chatting away with Quentin, she hadn't even noticed him standing there in the shadow of the open apartment doorway. Quentin noticed him before Katie did and came to an abrupt halt in the hallway.

"You really didn't need to escort me all the way to the door…" Her voice trailed off when she realized James was no longer beside her. Halting abruptly, she turned and saw that he'd stopped several steps behind her. Quentin's gaze was focused on something behind her. Following his gaze, she pivoted slowly and could make out a large shadow standing in an open doorway. Cain.

"That will be all, Quentin." Cain's voice was quiet, but he feared the underlying anger could be heard.

"Very good, sir." Quentin gave Katie a rueful smile before turning back towards the elevator.

Katie looked confused, having caught the underlying tension between the two men. She gave Cain a quick glance before walking back towards Quentin. "Thanks for the ride, James. I had a lot of fun on the drive over in the limo."

A soft smile crossed his rugged face. "You're more than welcome." Shooting Cain a defiant look, he reached into his pocket and produced a white business card. Reaching out, he tucked it in the pocket of her jacket. "Call me anytime if you need a ride. Day or night."

Katie reached out and squeezed his arm. "Thank you, James." Her voice was as gentle as the smile that crossed her face, and she stood there watching as the elevator door opened and Quentin stepped on board. He tipped his hat to Katie as the door closed.

Finally they were alone together, but the smile left Katie's face and she turned to him with a scowl. "What was that all about?"

"What was what about?"

"Don't play dumb with me, Cain. Why are you angry? I couldn't help running late, you know. I do have a job. Maybe we should just forget the whole thing." Katie turned and flounced back towards the elevator and stabbed at the button.

"I was jealous." The quiet admission seemed to startle her.

"Of what?" She looked completely baffled and Cain realized then that her innate charm was part of her personality and that Katie would draw people to her simply by virtue of being herself. There was a genuine quality about her. Her interest in people was real and everyone around her sensed that and responded to it. Him included.

"Never mind." He didn't like feeling this uncertain about anything and especially not about a woman. "Please come inside." He stepped back inside the apartment, held the door open, and waited to see what she would do.

Hesitantly, she followed him inside before her natural sense of humor reasserted itself and she laughed. "I feel like I'm being invited into Dracula's castle. Yes, I am entering freely and of my own will." The hallway had been shrouded in shadow with only a small night-light to illuminate it. The foyer was no different. It was just as dark and gloomy. "Didn't you pay your utility bill?

"I like the dark." Cain was not about to explain his choices to Katie. She could take him or leave him, but he was what he was. He stood far back from the light and watched her from the darkness.

Sensing his discomfort, she took off her coat and hung it next to his on the huge coat rack by the door. "That's all right. I don't mind the dark." The way she said it had a double meaning and he hoped she meant what she said. Once he made her his, there would be no going back for either of them.

She slipped her purse over the hook and tugged self-consciously on her sweater, waiting to see what he would do next. He laughed ruefully. "I haven't been much of a host so far, have I?"

"Not really," she teased him back.

"I'll do better." Extending his hand into the light, he enticed her forward. "Good evening, Katie. You look beautiful tonight." The blush that covered her cheeks started him wondering if it covered her entire body. Picturing her breasts a rosy pink made his entire body clench with desire.

Katie looked around inquiringly. "Where's Gabriel?"

As though he'd heard his name being called, Gabriel skittered down the hallway, his toenails clicking against the hardwood floor. He slid to a halt in front of Katie and looked up at her expectantly.

Katie laughed and crouched down in front of him. Gabriel was in dog heaven as she scratched his head and neck and he emitted a moan of doggy ecstasy. Pleased by his reaction, Katie tussled with the dog a few moments longer.

She was so beautiful and unselfconscious playing in the hallway with his dog. Cain decided that if he didn't do something, she'd stay there all night with the beast. "Gabriel, go." At his command, the dog glared at him for a moment before sulking off to the kitchen for his own supper.

"What is this strange mutinous effect you have on my staff?" he asked her.

"I have no idea what you're talking about." Katie stood and straightened her clothing, picking a stray dog hair off her pants leg.

The smile on her face and the glow in her eyes made him want to strip her bare and take her right in the damn foyer. His body tightened at the thought. Dinner first, he repeated silently to himself.

"Join me for dinner." It was a command and she responded by placing her hand in his. The sense of triumph he felt almost overwhelmed him as he tightened his hold on her hand and tucked it into the crook of his arm.

Cain was glad of the dark, as his cock had responded instantly to her, lengthening and swelling until his pants felt tight and uncomfortable. He was more than ready and willing to take her now. He knew the look on his face was one of carnal desire, and if she could see his face she would probably run screaming back to the safety of her own home. But she had stepped willingly into his world, and he was not willing to let her go.

"Where are we going?" Her voice trembled slightly as she spoke and Cain realized his silence was making her nervous.

"It's a surprise, but one I think you'll like. Trust me." As soon as he said the words he knew they were true. He wanted her trust. If she trusted him, she would open herself totally to him in bed. Without that trust, she would hold parts of herself back. And he wanted all of her.

She squeezed his hand in assent and allowed him to lead her down the hallway and up another set of stairs. Opening the door at the top, he ushered her into the rooftop conservatory. He watched as she took in the sight before her, sensing her enjoyment and seeing it through her eyes.

Lush green trees and plants of all shapes and sizes filled the glass-enclosed area, illuminated by rows of small twinkling lights. In the center of the room a small stone pool with a waterfall gurgled cheerfully. The air was alive with the smells of lavender, roses, and other assorted flowers.

Katie glided to the center of the room and turned in a slow circle, taking in every inch of the room. "This is absolutely beautiful."

He felt her enjoyment as if it were a living thing. The glow in her eyes and the softness on her face made him want to strip her naked and bury himself inside her warmth. Taking a deep breath, he strolled to the far corner of the room, carefully keeping to the shadows as he did so.

A wrought iron table, softly lit by a white pillar candle, was set for two with fine china and linen. Beside the table was a sideboard with a variety of covered dishes. Dinner awaited their pleasure. He pulled out one of the chairs and the noise made her glance to where he now stood. Hurrying over she surveyed the table.

"Your worries are over."

Her comment took him off-guard. "What worries?"

"I'm sure I'll like dinner. I'm enjoying myself. And, I'm sure I'll want to see you again." She ticked the points off on her fingers as she spoke, and he smiled, remembering their earlier conversation.

Chuckling, he seated her at the table, making sure the good side of his face was the one she could see. "Well, my mind is at ease now, and I can relax and enjoy the evening."

His amusement faded away as he stared down at her. She licked her lips and then glanced down at the empty china plate. He could see her tugging at the hem of her sweater. God, she looked good enough to eat. Food first, he reminded himself.

The wine had already been opened, so he filled two long-stemmed crystal glasses with the pale white liquid and handed one to her. She sipped nervously, the wine making her lips glisten. Leaning forward so that he was blocking the flickering light, he licked her lips. The taste of the crisp wine and the heat of her lips were intoxicating.

Reaching behind him, he removed the cover from one of the dishes. Plucking a chocolate-covered strawberry from the plate, he held it to her lips. He didn't allow her to eat it, but just ran the berry over her lips. Her tongue came out to taste it. "Suck the chocolate off."

She smiled seductively and then her tongue curled around the chocolate coating. If he'd been hard a few minutes ago, he now felt like he was going to burst. Images of her doing the same thing to his cock were making him sweat. His entire body screamed at him to take her. Now.

"Are we having dessert first?" Her lips surrounded the lush berry and she sucked it right out of his hands. Chewing the delectable treat, she moaned like a woman in the throes of an orgasm.

Suddenly, he could wait no longer. Dropping to one knee beside her, he cupped her face in his large hands and brought it towards him. Lightly brushing her eyelids with his thumbs, he waited until they closed, and then he leaned forward and brushed her lips with his.

So soft. That was his only thought. He went back for another taste. The flavors of chocolate, strawberry, and tart white wine all mingled on her mouth. His tongue traced her lips, licking at them until she parted them and moaned. Responding immediately, he thrust his tongue inside her mouth and explored every crevice. He rubbed her tongue and sucked it, all the while, never losing his grip on her face. Cain tasted the sweetness of her mouth and knew he had never tasted anything so fine in his entire life.

Reluctantly withdrawing from her mouth, he placed kisses all over her face before he pulled back into the shadows. "I want you." His voice was harsh even to his own ears.

"All right." Her whisper was barely audible.

He dragged his hand through his hair. "I need you now. Fast." His breathing was rough, but he held on to his control. Just. "Later I'll go slow. I promise." He wanted to be sure she understood what she was agreeing to.

"Yes."

Her reply was stark in the quiet of the night. The only other sound he could hear above his own rough breathing and the pounding of his heart was the gurgle of the fountain. Abruptly, he rose and scooped her off her chair all in one motion. His arms were like steel around her and there was no longer any chance he'd let her go. Dinner could wait. He would have his dessert first.

Keeping to the shadows, he carried her down the stairs, not stopping until he entered his bedroom. Kicking the door closed behind him, he let her legs slide down his body until she was standing in front of him with his arms still locked around her.

Chapter Eight

Katie lost all ability to breathe when Cain swept her up into his embrace and carried her from the rooftop garden. She caught glimpses of his harsh features as he passed quickly through the apartment. His green eye glittered like that of some wild animal on the hunt. Knowing she was the prey made her slightly nervous.

Cain was a huge man, and with a black leather patch over his left eye and his long black hair covering half of his face, he could easily be taken for a pirate. Picturing him in tight breeches and a leather vest swinging a cutlass on the deck of a ship was no problem. She wondered half hysterically if he'd make her walk the plank if she didn't perform to his liking. The solid thud of him kicking a door closed behind him gave her a sense of finality. There was no going back now. And, truthfully, she didn't think she wanted to.

Her legs were shaking as he released them and she clung to his shoulders for support. She was shivering both from fear and arousal. She suddenly realized that she'd put her sexuality in the deep freeze after the whole fiasco with Kent. Cain was the only man since then who'd been able to thaw her. The problem was he not only thawed her, he made her red-hot. That meant that Cain was becoming important to her. And, unfortunately, that gave him power over her.

His hands glided down her back and cupped her behind before pulling her closer and rubbing her against his rock-hard arousal. Her body responded instantly and she could feel the wetness and the ache between her legs. It didn't seem to matter if she wanted to lose control to Cain. He was going to wrest it from her.

"I'm going to fuck you, then I'm going to make love to you," he whispered in her ear as he bent to run his tongue around the edge. His tongue flicked inside her ear for a moment, and she shivered and clung to him.

"What's the difference?" Desperately, she tried to retain control. But Cain was busily licking and nipping at her neck and she arched her throat back to give him better access.

"There is a difference, but you'll like both," he promised hotly. He pulled back and his eye glittered in the faint light from the window as he reached out and slid her sweater off. Tossing it over his shoulder, he tugged her silk shirt from the waistband of her pants. Not giving her any time to object, the shirt followed her sweater to the floor.

She stood there feeling vulnerable in her bra and slacks, but allowed him to look at her. Raising his hands to her bra, he covered the white lace with his hands, which looked big and rough next to the delicate fabric. Molding her breasts with his fingers, he teased the nipples through the fabric. They were hard nubs, aching for more. Pushing them more firmly into his hands, she silently begged for more.

"Yes," he murmured as he unhooked the front clasp of her bra. He tugged it off and immediately reached for the waistband of her wool slacks. The zipper made a hissing noise as he lowered it and then dragged both her slacks and her panties down together.

Before she could contemplate her nakedness, he picked her up and sat her on the end of his bed. Boots, pants, and underwear were pulled away and she was left naked on the end of his bed.

"Beautiful," he muttered as he stood back to look at her.

Her arms came up to cover her breasts in a reflexive action, but he wasn't having any of that. "No, Katie." Gently, he tugged her hands away. "I want to see your breasts."

He urged her up further on the bed until her head was on the pillows and he was sitting next to her. Stroking his hands over her arms, he devoured her with his good eye. Taking his time, he ran his fingers lightly over her collarbone, dipping into the hollow just above it. Returning to the center of her chest, he drew a line with one finger to the point between her breasts. He made little circles with his finger, gradually expanding them until he was tracing a figure eight around her breasts, but not touching them.

Having his hands so close to her breasts but not touching them was torture, and she sighed in relief when he finally palmed her breasts. He seemed enthralled as he shaped and squeezed them in his hands. Katie had never been well-endowed, but Cain made her feel like the sexiest woman on the face of the planet. He teased her nipples between his thumb and forefinger, seeming pleased when she moaned and arched her back in pleasure.

"Cain." She reached for him, wanting him with her. It was a shock when he grabbed her hands, raised them over her head, and clasped them around two slats on the headboard. He wrapped them tightly around the hard wood, and he made sure she had a good grip before sliding his hands back down her arms.

"Don't move your hands," he whispered. "I want you to let me do whatever I want to you." Leaning over he kissed her gently on the lips. Her hands came away from the headboard to hold him close, but he clasped them firmly and returned them to the headboard.

"We've been through this before. If you can't do it on your own, I'll have to help you." He opened the drawer on the table next to the bed and withdrew a long black scarf. He teased her breasts with the end of the silk making her nipples pucker even tighter.

Katie knew what he was silently asking of her and she hesitated. Her only experience with this kind of game had been the other night in the park, and that had been incredibly intense. Only in her fantasies had she ever considered giving up control to a man by allowing him to tie her to the bed while he made love to her.

It was both frightening and arousing at the same time. Yet, there was an element of freedom in bondage. If she was tied to the bed, then she would have to accept whatever pleasure he allowed her. Everything was up to him. The only question was did she want to relinquish control to him again? Did she trust him enough to play this game again now that she understood what it entailed?

Cain watched her patiently as all her emotions played across her face. She knew he could tell when she'd made up her mind, as a small smile crossed his face before he reached up and carefully wrapped the silk around her wrists then the headboard. When he was finished, he stood. She tested the restraints, and though they weren't tight, she was securely tied to the bed.

With her arms over her head, her breasts were thrust up as an offering to him. And Cain, he just stood back and surveyed her naked body like some satisfied sultan. His body was still, but incredibly tense and it was with some shock that she realized he was still completely dressed.

"Take off your clothes, Cain." She wanted him in bed with her so she wouldn't feel so vulnerable.

"Make me." At her puzzled look, he elaborated. "Entice me. Spread your legs and show me you want me." His voice was thick with desire. "Offer yourself to me."

Katie struggled between her mounting desire and the fear of losing any more control to this dominant man. Something in his eyes almost pleaded with her to comply, as if he needed her to completely surrender to her desire for him.

Gathering her courage, she spread her legs wide apart and looked him straight in the eye. "Take off your clothes."

"Wider," he taunted.

Spreading her legs as wide as possible, she planted her feet on the mattress and arched her back. She was open wide to him now. He could see her sex glistening with arousal and waiting for him.

"Do you want me now?" she goaded him, wanting him as out of control as she was.

He swore savagely in the darkness and she heard the sound of a drawer being jerked open. Then came the sound of a packet being opened and a zipper being lowered. She knew he was sheathing himself in a condom, but he still was fully dressed.

Feeling wanton and bold, she taunted him with her womanly power. "I'm waiting," she purred as she arched her hips again.

"Fuck, yes," was his reply as he crawled up the bed and over her. Grabbing her knees with his hands, he held her wide open as he pushed his pulsing cock inside her.

He was so large she didn't know how she would take him. She tensed as he pushed forward, waiting for him to thrust deep, but he inserted just the tip and rocked himself slowly in and out of her. As she relaxed, he slid deeper inside her.

"That's it," he crooned. "You can take all of me. I know you can." He continued to rock into her a little more each time. "Hold on tight to the bed and relax." His voice was almost hypnotic as he spoke and she found herself responding to his instructions.

She had no control over the depths of his strokes as he kept her legs bent and spread wide. He looked large and slightly wild above her and she reveled in the fact that this big, dangerous, gorgeous man wanted her. It made her feel powerful and daring, and she thrust her hips up, daring him to go deeper.

As if she had finally unleashed the sleeping giant, he thrust himself to the hilt and although she had encouraged him to do it, she found it a little uncomfortable. But he was relentless and held himself deep inside her.

"Good girl," he soothed. "I knew you could take me." Placing her feet firmly against his shoulders, he then slid his hands down her legs, and around to her bottom. Squeezing both cheeks, he got a good grip on her. "I love your tight ass. Soon, I want you on your hands and knees with your ass in the air as I fuck you."

She had no time to think about that promise as he began to plunge in and out of her. Slowly at first and then harder and faster. Every time he thrust forward, her knees were pushed towards her head. Katie hung on to the headboard as Cain pounded in and out of her body. There was no room left for anything but Cain as he filled her body and her mind completely.

Gripping her bottom with one hand he pushed the other hand between their joined bodies and flicked her clitoris with one of his fingers. Katie could feel her entire body tighten from the top of her head to the soles of her feet. Her inner muscles clamped down hard on his thrusting cock and he moaned and thrust harder all the while his fingers worked their magic.

"Come for me, Katie." His voice was uneven as he continued to work her body.

Katie had no other thought in her head except completion. Being totally open to Cain and having him control their lovemaking made her even hotter. She tried to move her hips as she writhed on the bed, but he kept the same hard, fast pace, not slowing or changing. She tugged on her bonds in a desperate attempt to be free so she could make him do what she wanted.

"Come for me," he repeated. "You're so close, baby."

Katie thought she'd go mad if she didn't come. Now. "More, Cain," she cried. She tilted her head back and clenched her teeth as he continued to stroke her clitoris. The tension built and the explosion came from deep within her. She screamed as her body contracted around his.

Cain never stopped but pushed her feet off his shoulders, wrapped his arms around her hips, and continued to pound her body. He came in one long shudder and then collapsed on top of her, burying his face between her breasts.

Katie's legs were sprawled wide open and she could feel the fabric of Cain's pants against her thighs. He raised his head up long enough to reach up, untie her hands from the headboard, and remove the black silk scarf from her wrists. Slowly, he drew her arms down to her sides, and dropped his head back to her chest. Her hands tunneled through his long, beautiful hair. The silky strands slipped easily through her fingers. He made a muffled sound, but didn't budge from his prone position.

Making no move to disturb him, Katie continued to play with his hair. His head was pillowed on her breast and she could feel his hot breath on her skin. Her nipples were hard, aching nubs. She could feel his penis quivering inside her and her own body responded as her inner muscles squeezed him tight.

She felt the rumbling in his chest before she heard his laugh. "I better clean up first before we go again." He pulled out of her and off the bed in one motion.

Unable to summon the energy to move, she lay there sprawled on the bed and watched as Cain removed the used condom and dumped it into a wastepaper basket that was tucked next to the bedside table. Since meeting Cain, she'd had new and exciting erotic experiences, one after another, but this one had taken her to an entirely new level. What they'd just done together had been the most amazing sexual experience of her entire life.

Her whole body was still vibrating from her amazing climax and she realized that she felt a warmth in her chest. It took her a moment to recognize the feeling. She felt happy and wrapped her arms around herself to hug the feeling tight.

Katie was still basking in the afterglow when Cain came back to stand beside the bed. "How do you feel, Katie?" Casting an immense shadow, he covered her in darkness.

"I feel wonderful." Her reply was more of a breathy sigh.

"Good. I'm glad." He released a breath he'd been holding. "Because I'm just getting started."

He shucked his pants and underwear and slowly unbuttoned the soft cotton shirt that he wore, but kept it on. "I want to do everything with you, Katie. I want to suck your tits until you come. I want to eat your pussy until you scream. I want you to suck on my dick until I come and then I want to fuck you again." His words made her squirm and he smiled when he noticed.

"My hot little Katie. Will you let me do that? Will you do that for me?"

Her reply came without thought. "Yes." She held her arms out to him. For the first time in her life she wanted everything. Craved it. Whatever pleased him. That was what she wanted him to do. Then she wanted her turn at him. The thought of that big, hard body at her command made her moan. Cupping her breasts in her hands she plumped them up and offered them to him.

Cain had never seen a more erotic sight in his life. The trust Katie showed him by lying there and offering herself to him took his breath away. She looked like a pagan sacrifice spread out on his bed. Every muscle of his body was clenched tight. His dick was already hard again. He hadn't recovered this quick since he was a teenager.

His words had been purposely crude and explicit as he described what he wanted from her. Inwardly, he admitted that he was testing her to see if she would turn away from the darker, rougher aspects of him. They existed whether he wanted them to or not. Better for her to know now than later. He shook his head and smiled. Not his Katie, she was made of tougher stuff than that. If a little light bondage hadn't frightened her away, then a few crude words certainly wouldn't.

Lowering himself to the bed next to her, he reached out and ran the tip of his finger over one of her taut nipples. "You look like a sexy slave girl offering herself up to her lord and master." Bending down he flicked the tip of her nipple with his tongue. "I like that."

He tongued one rigid peak and then leaned over to play with the other one. He teased her until she was moaning and squirming. "Do you want more?"

"Yessss." Her legs moved restlessly on the mattress.

"Tell me what you want." Blowing gently on one wet nipple, he watched her as she moaned louder and the peak of her breast grew even tighter.

"Suck them, please."

"Such a polite little slave girl, you are. Are you sure that's what you really want?" he teased.

In response, she grabbed his hair and dragged him back to her breast. "I guess you're sure." Cain rewarded her by tugging one ripe, rosy nipple into his mouth. He teased the tip with his tongue before nibbling at it with his teeth. Then without warning, he began to suck.

He feasted on her breasts, first one than the other. Back and forth, he licked and sucked, teased, and taunted until Katie was thrashing like a wild woman on the bed.

His cock was hard and throbbing so he spread her legs with his thighs and pushed it against the hard nub of her clit. Her hips moved up and down as she used his cock to pleasure herself. God, she was hot.

He continued stimulating her tits with both his mouth and his hands. His cock was wet with her arousal as she continued to stroke herself on her dick. He could feel the heat of her throbbing pussy as it moved over his length, and for a second, he thought he was going to come on her stomach.

Every muscle in his body was screaming for release, but he wouldn't give in. Not yet. He turned every ounce of his attention to making Katie come. Finally, he was rewarded when she stiffened and began to convulse on the bed.

A low, long squeal filled the air as she came and Katie covered her mouth with her hands as if to try and keep her orgasm silent. He was having none of it. Reaching up, he tugged her hands away. "I want all of it. I want to feel it, to see it, to touch it, to taste it and to smell it. Everything, Katie. Give me everything."

Katie indeed gave him everything and when she was finally lying limp on the bed, Cain amused himself by blowing lightly on the turgid peaks. He pushed his dick hard against her leg for some relief, but he wasn't finished playing with her yet.

"Well, that's one."

"One what?" Katie asked in a sleepy, confused voice.

"That's the first thing I said I wanted to do to you." He ran one finger around her nipple and then trailed it down her stomach to her navel. Leaning over, he trailed his lips over her open mouth. Her lips raised and opened to him of their own accord, and her pink tongue flicked out to taste his. He shuddered for a moment, enjoying her playfulness.

"I sucked your tits until you came," he reminded her. "Now, I'm going to eat your pussy until you come again." Her eyes widened in surprise as he moved lower down on the mattress. "You didn't think I'd forget my promise, did you?"

Turning her body slightly sideways, he found a comfortable position on his side. No matter how he turned her, he couldn't see her in the pale light. Sighing, he sat up and moved to sit by her head. "We have a problem."

"What." Katie reached out and stroked his arm all the way down to his hand. "You're still wearing your shirt." Now she sounded perplexed.

"That's the problem. I want to turn on the light and look at you. To be able to take off my shirt and enjoy myself." He reached over the side of the bed and picked up the familiar long black scarf.

"I don't understand."

He folded the scarf in half lengthwise and held it loosely in both hands. "I want to blindfold you so you can't see me. It will be better for both of us that way." He trailed the silk scarf over her belly and then her breasts.

Katie shivered as the fabric tugged on her sensitive nipples. Her hands gripped the sheets tight. Sensing her hesitation, he used the scarf to tease her breasts again. "You'll find even greater pleasure if you rely on your remaining senses," he promised. "It will heighten your response."

Sensing her uncertainty, he bent forward and kissed her. It was a long, lingering kiss full of promise. When he pulled away, Katie gave a little moan of distress. "Please, for me." Softly, he kissed her lips, her cheek, her eyes. "You liked what I did to you earlier," he reminded her.

Katie gave him a hesitant nod and he wasted no time pulling her into a sitting position. Wrapping the length of cloth around her head several times before tying it in the back, he then turned her in the bed until her head was near the bottom and her feet were facing the headboard.

The click of the light switch made her jump, but other than that she made no move. Like a deer caught in the blinding glare of headlights she couldn't even see, Katie seemed frozen in place.

"You're like a fantasy." Cain tore off his shirt and flung it to the floor, never taking his eyes off her pearly white body.

Her eyes were obscured behind the black blindfold, but her cheeks were pink and her lips were slightly swollen from his kisses. A small bite mark was evident on one shoulder and he felt an almost savage pleasure that he'd marked her as his. Her nipples were distended and cherry red after all the attention he'd given them and made a luscious sight against the pale skin of her breasts.

Getting comfortable between her legs, he bent forward and took a deep breath, inhaling her enticing scent. "You smell hot and sexy." His finger traced a line up the inside of one smooth, white thigh and then through the soft hair covering her mound. "It's curly," he noted. "In my fantasy it was straight, but this is so much better."

"Did you dream of me?" Katie's breathing was getting more rapid. He could see the pulse fluttering in her neck as her arousal grew.

"Dreaming of you is all I've done lately. But what about you? Did your dreams include being spread out for my pleasure while I explore you at my leisure?" He continued to comb through the dark hair, coming close but never touching her clitoris.

"I asked about *your* dreams. What do you want?" She raised her arms over her head and arched her body towards him. Katie was as seductive as any siren, luring him onward.

Trailing his tongue up the inside of her thigh, he paused and nuzzled her pubic hair. "I want to taste you. To pleasure you."

His tongue flicked out and circled the nub of her arousal. Her hips rose to meet his mouth and he caught her clit gently between his teeth and flicked it softly. Katie moaned and thrust her hips higher.

Giving it one final flick, he licked the soft, slick folds of her opening. She was so pink and wet and his. He took a deep breath and knew if he weren't careful he'd come on the damn sheets. Katie turned him on like no other woman ever had.

Continuing his exploration of her soft slick flesh, he slowly inserted a finger inside her, not stopping until it was buried to the hilt. She writhed on the bed, trying to coax him to move his finger.

"Cain!" she wailed when he kept his finger still inside her. Instead, he slowly pushed another finger inside to join the first. She wailed again as her hips lifted off the mattress.

"Hold still, Katie." He blew on her heated flesh as he watched her body flush.

"I can't," she muttered. "Do something."

Cain began to slowly move his fingers within her while at the same time finding her clit and beginning to suck on it. This time he didn't stop. Starting slow at first, he built a steady rhythm until Katie's head was thrashing from side to side, her hands fisted in the sheets. Her hips pumped wildly in the air as she encouraged him.

"God, yes. More. Again." Katie gasped out as she continued to reach for release. Her breathless entreaties spurred him on.

Pushing his fingers all the way inside her hot, wet body, he tongued her clit and was rewarded when he felt her inner muscles clench around his fingers.

He didn't let up, but kept up the steady pressure even as Katie started screaming her release. When she was finished, he slowly removed his fingers and nuzzled her sensitive skin. Stroking her legs and her stomach, he waited patiently until she was relaxed once again.

"That was amazing." Katie sounded well satisfied and that pleased him greatly.

Moving up slightly on the bed, he kissed her stomach and her breasts and finally he placed a soft kiss on her lips. "Taste how sexy you are." Running the two fingers that he'd used to make her come along her lips, he waited for her to taste herself.

Her tongue flicked out and ran down the length of one finger making him groan. Pushing his dick against her soft stomach to help ease the ache, he waited to see what she would do next.

Capturing both fingers in her mouth, she licked and sucked them both. "Mmm. Good," she moaned.

She was killing him, but there was no way he was going to stop her. He ground his arousal against her body and allowed her to do as she wished.

Easing her fingers out of her mouth, she surprised him with her request. "That's number one and two. Isn't it time for number three?"

Cain pulled away from her and bolted upright, gasping for air. The image of her taking him in her mouth and sucking him almost made him come right there and then. He ran both hands through his hair and desperately tried to regain control. Katie didn't help matters any as she continued to run her feet up and down his flanks while he sat back and stared at her enticing body.

"Well, isn't it my turn?" she teased him with a saucy smile on her face. When he didn't respond immediately, she began to frown and look concerned. "Cain?"

Reaching out, he lifted one of her hands to his lips and kissed her palm before placing it against his cheek. "Everything is all right, but we may have to skip that one and go right to the last one. I don't think I'd last a minute with your sexy mouth on my cock." How was that for honesty?

"Okay. We can always do that later." Katie opened her arms to him and he was lost.

"Let me love you, Katie." Stretching out beside her, he placed frantic kisses on her upturned face.

"That's not what you said you wanted earlier." Katie tried to wrap her arms around his shoulders, but he captured them and held them in one of his hands. Slowly, he lifted them over her head.

"Forget what I said earlier. Earlier, I was being an ass." Cain took Katie's mouth in a long, hot kiss. He didn't just kiss her. He devoured her. Wanting—no, needing—to please her, give back to her, and take from her.

"Love me, Cain," Katie demanded.

"Hell, yes." He jerked up in the bed, grabbed a condom, and sheathed himself in record time. Quickly, he burrowed between her legs and thrust himself inside her waiting warmth.

Where he'd been frantic before, now that he was inside her, something deep inside him relaxed. He bent all his considerable skill towards arousing Katie all over again. Kissing her delectable lips and her luscious breasts was like indulging in a veritable feast. His senses filled with the scent and taste of Katie.

And Katie responded as if she had been made especially for him. Her arousal was almost instantaneous and in only moments she was meeting his thrusts and kissing whatever part of him she could reach. Lifting her head, she lightly bit his shoulder and he lost all control.

Like a madman, he thrust into her. His balls tightened and then came blessed release. He continued to thrust until he had emptied himself into her and then he collapsed, taking care not to crush her beneath him.

Cain didn't know how much time had passed when he finally gained enough energy to move. It was only then that he realized Katie was gently rubbing his hair and his shoulder. He closed his eyes, swallowed hard, and gave thanks that it was his good shoulder and not his scarred one.

Reluctantly, he withdrew from her body and her embrace. Katie treated him with a tenderness that he'd never had in his entire life. If he weren't careful, she'd make him weak and then where would he be? His resolve hardened and he pulled back from her.

"Come back." She held her arms out to him.

"I need to clean up first." He knew his voice was harsh when she flinched slightly and dropped her hands. Unable to bear her withdrawal from him, he softened his rejection by dropping a kiss on her stomach.

"But let's get you comfortable first." Reaching behind him, he clicked off the light and plunged the room back into darkness. It took a moment for his eye to adjust and then he lifted Katie until her back was turned to him. Kissing her neck, he unwound the blindfold and returned it to the nightstand.

Guiding her to the pillows, he tucked her in before leaving her. "I'll be back in a minute."

"I'll be here."

In the bathroom, Cain disposed of the used condom and cleaned himself up with a warm washcloth. Bracing both arms on the counter, he stared at his reflection in the dim light from the night-light. "You're a hard bastard, Benjamin." He nodded at his reflection in agreement. But even knowing that, he knew there was no way he would let Katie go. He would do everything in his power to tie her to him, to make her want to stay with him, but there was no way he would be able to give up any control to her. It had to be his way or no way.

Having shored up his defenses, he tugged on a shirt that had hung on the back of the bathroom door. Taking a lukewarm damp washcloth with him, he returned to the bed and ran the cloth all over Katie's body, making her more comfortable. Crawling in behind her sleepy form, he pulled her close, wrapping both arms around her warm body.

"Sleep," he whispered in her ear. Katie responded by snuggling closer to him, automatically curling into his body like she'd been doing it for years. She fit him perfectly. But it was more than that. Katie felt right lying here in his arms and in his bed. It was if this woman had been fashioned especially for him. That thought was both exhilarating and worrisome at the same time.

Katie moved restlessly in her sleep, so he gathered her closer and whispered reassuringly in her ear. She responded immediately to his voice, cuddling closer to him. Making a pillow out of his chest, she finally sank into a deep sleep. Her breath stirred the hairs on his chest, and it wasn't long before he was painfully aroused again.

His cock twitched against the sheet, but he made no move to wake Katie. She was obviously exhausted from the unaccustomed sexual activity, and he figured she was probably a little sore. Instead, he just enjoyed the feel of her against his body. He held her there in the dark for several hours not willing to risk losing any of his time with her to sleep.

An hour before dawn, he reluctantly dragged himself out of bed and gathered her clothing together. Laying it all on the bed, he stood there and took one final lingering look at her. When he'd risen, she'd rolled over and snuggled into his pillow, as if seeking his warmth. Bending over, he kissed her awake and told her to get dressed.

He sensed her sleepy confusion as she slowly dressed, but he ignored it and pulled on his own clothes. Wrapping his arms around her, he ushered her into her coat and down the elevator to the garage. As per his instructions of the previous night, Quentin had the limo waiting outside. Unable to resist, Cain wrapped Katie in his arms and pulled her close to his chest for one final hug.

"I'll be away for a few days. Be good while I'm gone." He held her face in his hands and gave her one last, hard kiss. "Miss me," he ordered as he settled her in the car.

It was only when the car had pulled away that Cain realized that Katie hadn't said a single word.

Chapter Nine

The next few days were up and down like a roller coaster for Katie. One moment, she was up, remembering the erotic night of lovemaking she and Cain had shared. The next, she was depressed and thinking about the way he ushered her out of his bed the next morning. She hadn't been able to look Quentin in the eye as he'd driven through the streets in the early morning light. Thankfully, he had sensed her discomfort and left her to her own thoughts.

Truthfully, she didn't know how she felt about their night together. They hadn't even eaten dinner before she'd allowed him to whisk her off to his bed. What they'd done in his bed still made her blush. A few weeks ago, she would never have thought she was the type to engage in sexual bondage games, much less enjoy them. Katie knew it was because she loved Cain, for her there was no other explanation. On the other hand, she had no idea if he had any feelings for her or if he just thought she was easy.

Her love for Cain had become apparent to her the morning Quentin had driven her home. She'd stumbled up the stairs and straight to bed. Emotionally, she had been a wreck. Alternately, she'd cried and cursed for an hour before dragging herself to the shower to get ready for work.

Whether she liked it or not, on some deep level she trusted Cain. Otherwise, she never would have allowed him to either bind her or blindfold her, and neither would she have given him complete access to her body. She had surrendered to him totally, emotionally and physically. Katie knew that she would only commit such a daring act for a man she loved.

Cain, on the other hand, seemed determined to keep her at a distance. The way he hid half his face from her in the light told her he didn't quite trust her. Tears came to her eyes when she recalled the way he had kept her from touching his bare skin. At this point she didn't know if it was because of some deformity or if he just didn't like to be touched. Either way, it hurt her. And the way he'd had his driver take her home, rather than taking her himself, had left her feeling unsure about the whole basis of their relationship. So far, she had done all the giving.

It wasn't that she'd hadn't talked to Cain since. No, quite the opposite in fact. That very evening when she'd stumbled home from work, he'd called her from wherever he was and he'd phoned her every evening since. He was interested in everything she did and asked her about her painting and about work at the coffee shop. It had taken her several nights to catch on to the fact that he never talked about himself.

All he would say was that he was away on business, but never once did he tell her exactly what he did. "I buy and sell things. Stocks, bonds, property, companies, and anything else I choose," he'd told her when she pressed. Then he'd changed the subject, making it clear that he had said all he was going to.

She asked him if he'd ever bought a building, hoping he could give her some advice to pass on to Lucas. So Katie had explained all about the building being sold and about Lucas having to find a new location. She poured out all her fears about what could happen to Lucas and to her job.

He listened quietly until she had finished and then answered her in the coldest voice she'd ever heard from him. "It's just the way business is done. The buyer is actually being very generous by letting the lease run until the end instead of just buying it out and evicting him from the premises." She still got shivers thinking about how remote and unreachable he'd seemed at that moment.

"That's exactly what Lucas said," she muttered into the receiver.

"Lucas understands that this is just business. It's not personal." Cain quickly ended the conversation and hung up, leaving Katie feeling even more disheartened.

Cain always seemed distracted and remote when he called. Lying in bed, thinking about their evening chats, it occurred to Katie that Cain had never told her if he was away on personal business or just regular business. She had just assumed it had something to do with his work because he never talked about his personal life. It disturbed her to know that she didn't even know if he had brothers or sisters or if his parents were still alive. He, on the other hand, knew about Lucas and about the death of her grandmother.

Cain had sent her four dozen roses and a note promising her a real dinner when he returned, but that was cold comfort for Katie. What she really wanted was for him to talk to her and to share some of the details of his life with her.

As much as she cared for him, Katie knew she needed more or her love would quickly shrivel and become resentment and hurt feelings. They would have to talk when he came back. She shivered in dread at the thought of Cain turning remote and cold as he dismissed her questions. If he decided not to talk, no force on earth would make him.

To take her mind off her troubles, she did what she'd always done. Katie painted. This latest picture of Cain showed him standing among the lush green of the rooftop garden. The table was set the same romantic way it had been the night she'd gone to his apartment. Lights twinkled merrily and the fountain trickled in the garden, Cain was half in and half out of the light. Part of him was buried in the shadows of the dense foliage while the patio lights illuminated the other half.

He looked strong and handsome in the painting and she had captured the intensity of his stare as he extended a large, sturdy hand to an unseen guest. Katie wasn't sure if he was entreating her to join him in the darkness or asking her help in pulling him from the darkness. She feared it was the former, but hoped it was the latter.

The completed painting joined the other two in the series and now the three of them were propped side by side against the wall. One scene flowed effortlessly into the next telling a story.

Now a blank canvas sat on her easel awaiting the final painting in the tale. Katie didn't know if the painting would be one of light or dark. Would Cain pull her completely into his dark world? Would she be able to coax him into the light? Or would they be destined to exist in that nether world half in and half out of the light? That was up to Cain. She felt that he had strong feelings towards her, and she desperately hoped her instincts were correct.

Thank heavens it was Thursday. Cain had been gone for just over a week and was due back tomorrow. He hadn't been sure what time he'd be home, but when they'd talked last night, he'd promised to call her. Whatever business was occupying him was not good. He'd been distracted every night he'd called and had been more terse than not. There had been no more playful bouts of phone sex, but she had done her best to lighten their phone calls by sharing bits and pieces of her day with him. In truth, he genuinely seemed to enjoy that part of their conversations.

Katie walked to work, enjoying the brisk morning air. The streets were coming alive as she left the apartment. Other people, like herself, who had to work early, had already started their day. The newsstand was opening as she passed by and she greeted Mr. Jenkins, the owner, as she strolled by. She smiled at a woman who was rushing to catch a bus, and waved at an elderly gentleman who was out for his daily walk. Some of the people she knew by name, but many she knew only by sight as they all appeared on the street at the same time every morning. Such was life in the city. She treasured her early morning amble to work, using the time to sort out her thoughts. The sights and sounds energized her and the crisp morning air invigorated her.

By the time she let herself in the coffee shop she was in a better frame of mind and ready for work. She'd been very careful this week, not wanting Lucas to find out about Cain yet. He would only worry about her and ask questions she just wasn't ready to answer. She knew he suspected she was seeing someone, but so far he had kept his own counsel.

"Good morning, Lucas." Keeping her voice upbeat, she breezed past him to the office to hang up her coat and put away her purse. The smell of cinnamon filled the air and her stomach growled as it anticipated a morning snack of fresh cinnamon buns drizzled with icing. Tying on a clean apron, she returned to the kitchen and started in on her morning routine by putting on a pot of coffee in the kitchen. When she glanced up, Lucas was staring at her.

"When are you going to tell me what's wrong, Katie?" Lucas's voice was not accusing, but she sensed the underlying hurt. Obviously, she hadn't concealed her emotional turmoil as well as she'd thought she had.

Going to him immediately, she wrapped her arms around his waist and leaned into his strength. "I thought I hid it so well."

She felt his kiss on the top of her head even as his arms came around her shoulders to comfort her. "Only to someone who doesn't know you. In truth, you've been distracted all week long, but things haven't been right since the day I told you I sold that damned painting." He sighed and released her. "I'm beginning to wish that I'd never put it in the window."

"Sometimes, I wish that too, but a wise man once told me that change was inevitable and it was how you dealt with it that mattered." She went over to the cupboard and pulled down two mugs. Expertly she tugged out the coffeepot and inserted one mug under the trickling brew while she filled the other cup by pouring coffee from the pot. When the other cup was full, she pulled it from the coffee machine and replaced the pot, all without spilling a drop. Returning to the counter, she plunked both coffees down and waited.

"Obviously, that guy didn't know what he was talking about." Lucas was chuckling at her, his smile brightening his whole face. "Only you would throw my own words back in my face." He picked up his mug and took an obviously much-needed gulp. Katie examined his face and noticed the circles under his eyes. He looked almost as bad as she did, but she'd been too wrapped up in her own worries to notice.

"Thanks for the coffee." He paused. "But seriously, Katie, what's wrong? Are you worried about the business? Is it some guy?"

Something in her expression must have tipped him off because his coffee cup made a thud as he slammed it to the counter. His large hands flattened on the countertop and he leaned towards her. "Did some guy hurt you?" Lucas's eyes glowed, promising immediate retribution.

"It is a guy. But he didn't hurt me, at least not in the way you mean." She paused to gather her thoughts.

Lucas was not reassured. "But he's done something that's upset you." It was a statement, not a question, and it demanded a response from her.

Tugging on the tails of her apron, she marshaled her thoughts. "I met this guy and it got pretty intense fast." Lucas waited impatiently for her to continue. His whole body practically vibrated with his barely contained energy. "I'm not sure he feels the same way I do and it worries me. That's all?" She hoped her condensed explanation would satisfy him, but one look at his face told her no such luck.

"That's all!" he roared. Lucas's hands curled into fists on the top of the counter. "Katie. You haven't even looked at a man since Kent and now you're telling me you're serious about some guy that I don't even know."

Katie knew it was that fact, more than any other, that both upset and hurt him at the same time. At times, Lucas took his role as big brother way too seriously for Katie's liking. This was obviously one of those times, so she tried to smooth it over just a little by offering him some reassurance. "But you do know him, in a way. It's the guy who bought the painting."

"I don't know him at all. I only dealt with his assistant, that Martha what's-her-name." Lucas started pacing in the kitchen. "How the hell did he meet you?"

"He followed me home," Katie replied in a meek voice. She braced herself for the explosion.

"He followed you home. My god, Katie, do you have a death wish? You don't know anything about this guy." Lucas was now frantically pacing back and forth across the kitchen but not once did he take his eyes off Katie.

She held her hands out pleadingly in front of her and tried to find the words to placate him. "He didn't approach me at first and he told me who he was immediately. We've spent some time together…" Her voice trailed off as Lucas rounded the counter and hauled her up in front of him. His grip was gentle even though his whole body was vibrating with barely suppressed anger.

"Katie, you've been spending time with a virtual stranger that none of your friends have met. Do you have any idea how dangerous that is?" He shook her lightly as he spoke.

Katie pulled back and put her hands on her hips. Now she was the one getting angry. "I'm a grown woman not a child. Besides which, I feel safe when I'm with him." She felt like stomping her foot in anger and would have if she hadn't just told Lucas she wasn't a child.

"It's the fact that you are a woman—a beautiful, young woman—that worries me." Lucas sighed and shook his head. "You know I'm going to worry about you until I meet him. At least tell me his name and let me check him out for you." Lucas smiled and added in a cajoling voice, "Then I won't worry so much." When that gambit looked like it might not work, he quickly added, "Katie, I don't need any more gray hair."

Katie burst out laughing, as he'd known she would. Lucas didn't have a gray hair on his head. It was still a thick blond that he kept chopped off short. She stepped forward and ruffled his hair. "We can't have that happen to your beautiful hair, can we? It's not a secret, I guess. His name is Cain Benjamin."

Lucas went as still as a statue. "What did you say?"

Katie began to get nervous. "Cain Benjamin. Why, do you know him?"

"Sit down, honey." He helped her sit on a stool and took both her hands in his, and the bleak look on his face began to frighten her.

"Just tell me what you know. You're scaring me."

"I'm the one who's scared, but you've got nothing to worry about. I'll take care of things."

"Take care of what? How do you know Cain?" Her voice was a high-pitched wail. She was very afraid of what Lucas was going to tell her.

Gripping her hands tight in his he took a deep breath and began. "I did some research on E. S. Investors."

Now Katie was perplexed. "What does that have to do with this?"

"This company buys and sells real estate, businesses, and just about any other thing it wants to." Katie was wondering why that phrase sounded so familiar and almost missed Lucas's next statement. "It's owned and operated by one man. Cain Benjamin."

"No, that's not possible." Katie felt all the blood drain from her face. Her head felt like it was spinning. She shook her head, the denial immediately springing to her lips. "You must be mistaken."

"I wish I was." He took her cold hands in his large, warm ones. Katie was glad for the warmth. Her whole body felt cold and she began to shake.

Lucas chafed her hands between his. "Reclusive multimillionaire, Cain Benjamin. He made a fortune on the Internet companies when they first started and is a wizard on the stock markets as well. Whatever he touches turns to gold, but he keeps to himself. I couldn't even find a picture of this guy online and he's been written up in every major business magazine."

The thought that Cain would simultaneously make love to her and destroy something he knew she loved was almost incomprehensible. Her laughter was bitter. He'd already known about Lucas losing the location for his shop. After all, he was the one taking it from him. Katie felt like a fool remembering how she'd poured her heart out to him over the phone. She shuddered when she remembered his cold reply. "It's business," he'd replied. And she guessed, to him that was what mattered. Her feelings certainly didn't seem to make any difference to him.

Lucas had released her hands and wrapped his arms around her, but Katie couldn't feel them. She couldn't feel anything at all. The sound of hysterical laughter filled the air and she wished whoever it was would shut up so she could think. Her whole body was shaking and she was chilled to the bone, so very, very cold.

"I know you're cold, honey." She was surprised when Lucas answered her. She hadn't realized she'd spoken out loud. "You've had a shock, but everything will be all right," his deep voice rumbled.

The world was a deep haze to her now and tears blurred her vision. The only solid thing in her world was Lucas and she clung to him for dear life. His voice coaxed her into her coat and in moments she was bundled into his car. For a moment, she came out of her funk, knowing something wasn't right.

"What about the shop? We have to open the shop." She had to make Lucas understand that it was time for work.

Both of his hands were clenched on the wheel, his knuckles white. "That's okay, baby. I'll open late today."

"But we never open late." She knew something was wrong, but she felt so tired and emotionally drained that, without realizing it, she drifted off to sleep. Katie woke briefly when the car stopped and Lucas lifted her out of the vehicle. But by the time he'd reached her apartment she was fast asleep in the safety of his arms.

Lucas took his time and tucked her into bed. He removed her shoes and tugged off her jeans before covering her with the comforter. He hadn't felt this kind of anger since he'd almost beaten his old man to death. Taking a deep cleansing breath, he looked at the angel sleeping on the bed. Anger wouldn't help her now, and he was too old to do something stupid and risk ending up back in prison. Sleep was the best thing for her now. The look on her face was not one he'd easily forget. She felt betrayed right to her very core and one man was to blame.

He crept out of the room to make a call. Judy would go in early and cover the shop until he could get back there. Picking up the receiver, he started to dial, only to come to a complete stop. Three paintings were propped up against the wall. Stark and beautiful, they told the story of her and Cain's relationship.

In the first one, he was an indistinct shadow lurking in the shadows. In the next one, she had painted him only half in the dark. His features were strong and harsh, yet he enticed her to come to him. And the final one was the most telling. The romantic setting was evident and Katie had painted him like some tragic figure, beckoning her to save him. Her feelings for him were evident in the final painting. It was in every brush stroke. Katie loved the bastard, even though it was evident to him that Cain had seduced her. And that made Lucas hate him even more.

Chapter Ten

Katie woke with a pounding in her head. Groaning, she rolled over and pulled the pillow over her head. Her mouth was dry and her eyes were gritty. It felt like she had a hangover but that was impossible since she never had more than one or two drinks at a time, and she certainly didn't remember drinking anything anyway. Peeking out from under the pillow, she glanced at the bedside clock. It was just after six.

Panic hit her and she rolled up in bed and planted her feet on the floor. She would be late for work if she didn't hurry. It was then she remembered everything from the day before. Burying her head in her hands, memories flooded her brain. The tense conversation between her and Lucas that ended with her discovery that Cain was the one forcing Lucas's coffee shop to relocate. Cain was the big, anonymous business buying the building.

Scrubbing her eyes with her fingers to clear out some of the sleep, Katie sat on the side of her bed and wondered what to do. It had been a shock to her system yesterday to realize just how much Cain was holding back from her. She had shared herself totally with him, while he kept most of himself hidden from her.

It was hard, facing the fact that she loved a man she didn't really know. All her instincts screamed that a good man lurked just under the façade. Katie just didn't know if she was the right woman to unearth him. Sighing, she knew it didn't really matter. She loved him so much that she had to try.

Yesterday, she had fallen to pieces. She wasn't proud of that fact, but it had happened and there was nothing to do now but move forward. After finally trusting enough to attempt a relationship with a man after so long, Cain's deception had hit her hard. And it was indeed a betrayal of sorts. She had poured out all her fears about what was happening with her job, and all the while he'd been the one controlling the outcome. It made her sad that he felt it necessary to hide it from her. Yes, she might be mad at him, but she would have tried to see his point of view.

With that in mind, Katie made a decision. Cain was expected back this evening and she would go to his place and talk to him. Maybe if she gave him an opening, he would tell her himself. Maybe he was just waiting for the right moment.

Shaking her head at her own foolishness, she raised her aching head and studied the forlorn-looking woman in the dresser mirror. "Maybe I'm just grasping at straws," she muttered.

Regardless, if they were to have any kind of relationship, there had to be no more lies or omissions. If she couldn't trust him then they truly had nothing and she would have to face the fact that she'd been mistaken about the kind of man Cain was.

The image in the mirror was pitiful, so she dragged herself out of bed. What she needed right now was a nice hot shower. She was still half-dressed, for heaven's sake. Stripping off her clothes, she dropped them on the floor. She rummaged around in her closet, pulled out her robe, and dragged it on. It was when she was heading for the bathroom that she saw the note taped to her bedroom door.

She recognized Lucas's handwriting as she pulled the sheet of paper off the door. The note was short and to the point. "I'll be by later to check on you." She read it aloud and thanked her lucky stars that she had such a loyal friend in Lucas.

Now, she really needed a shower. Lucas would not be happy with her decision to talk to Cain, but it was something she had to do. This relationship was worth fighting for and she would not give up yet. Katie needed to reassure Lucas that yesterday's meltdown was only due to the shock of the moment and fatigue, and that she was strong enough to survive if things didn't work out with Cain. It would be painful, but if life had taught her only one thing, it was that life went on regardless of heartbreak.

Padding to the shower, she began to practice what she would say to both Cain and Lucas. Both men were difficult and needed to be approached carefully. It was going to be a long day.

Katie was nervous as she stood in front of the large steel door. The wind whistled through the air and penetrated her coat as she contemplated the private entrance to Cain's building. There was a buzzer to one side that she had yet to push. She'd just finished dealing with one difficult man and now here she was planning to deal with another one. She wasn't sure if she was incredibly brave or just a glutton for punishment. At the moment, it was a toss-up.

Lunch with Lucas had been challenging, to say the least. It had been incredibly sweet of him to show up at her apartment with a selection of sandwiches and treats. His only concern, at first, had been getting her to eat something. Yesterday's episode had left him feeling very protective of her. So she'd allowed him to sit her at the table and ply her with good food. When they had both eaten, she'd told him that she planned to confront Cain.

Lucas had not taken her decision well. He'd been visibly upset by her decision, and it had taken her the better part of an hour to calm him down enough to understand that she was going to do this whether he wanted her to or not. Lucas wanted to confront Cain, but Katie was having none of that. She was an adult and had to handle this on her own.

It hadn't been easy, but eventually he had succumbed to her powers of persuasion, and reluctantly accepted her decision. He had stubbornly extracted her promise that she would call him the moment she got home. No matter what time it was.

Wiping her damp palms against her jeans, she plucked up her courage and pushed the buzzer. She waited. And waited. And waited. No one answered. She leaned her finger on the buzzer again and kept it pressed there a full twenty seconds. Faint barking could be heard in the background.

"Who is it?" Cain's voice boomed loudly from the speaker. He sounded extremely annoyed.

Katie swallowed hard and then cleared her throat. "It's me." When he was silent, she glared at the speaker. "Katie."

"I know who it is," he growled. "Wait there, I'll be down in a minute."

Katie tapped her foot nervously and rubbed her hands up and down her arms. She was shivering and it was as much nerves as it was cold. Tugging the strap of her purse higher on her shoulder, she willed the door to open. Finally, after what seemed like ages, the door was pulled partially open.

"Come inside." Katie obeyed the stark command and slid through the small opening. The door slammed shut behind her and she found herself in total darkness.

She could feel Cain standing beside her, a solid presence in the pitch-black parking garage. "I'm beginning to think you really are a vampire," she muttered. She bit her lip to keep herself from speaking again. Why did she always make stupid jokes when she was nervous? Cain said nothing, but took her by the hand and led her towards the elevator. Katie followed blindly in his wake.

"Why are you here? I was going to call you later." The elevator door slid open and he tugged her inside.

She wasn't really surprised when the light was extremely dim. Cain was nothing more than a large hulking shape. His body was a solid presence behind her, and it took all her resolve to keep herself erect. All she wanted to do was lean back against him and absorb his strength, his scent, and indeed his very essence.

"I missed you." Her voice was low and intimate in the small confines of the ascending elevator.

His huge sigh actually ruffled her hair and then his arms enveloped her from behind, his chin coming to rest on the top of her head. She felt surrounded by him and closed her eyes to enjoy the sensation.

Tears came to her eyes, as she knew that this might be the last time this would happen. If Cain refused to talk to her, to be honest with her, then she would not be seeing him again. Not if she wanted to retain her self-respect. Katie wanted to freeze this moment in time, but the elevator came to a halt.

Cain said nothing as the elevator opened. The door to his apartment was open and a lady was leaving. Katie's heart stopped for a moment before she recognized Martha Jones, the lady who had bought the painting from Lucas.

"I'll be going if there's nothing else, Mr. Benjamin." Martha had a leather folder clutched tight in her arms. She waited until Cain nodded at her and then turned to Katie and gave her a quick glance that was filled with something that looked like pity. "Have a good evening then, sir. Good evening, Miss Wallace." Martha hurried to the elevator and disappeared behind the closing door.

Before Katie could even begin to wonder what that exchange was all about, Cain ushered her through the front door of his apartment. The door closed with a solid thud. There was no going back now.

The foyer was dark but she could sense Cain leaning towards her. He cupped her chin in his hand and kissed her gently. She leaned into the kiss, loving the warm solid feel of his lips sliding across hers. For a moment, all the anger and doubts of the day before just melted away. There was only Katie and Cain. Nothing else existed. Katie believed that Cain had to feel the magic just as much as she did. Her bag fell to the floor unnoticed as she wrapped her arms around him and kissed him back with all the love she felt.

"I love you." The words tumbled from her mouth even as her brain screamed at her to stop. She wanted to recall the words the moment they left her mouth, but once said, they could not be taken back. He froze immediately, his entire body turning to stone in her embrace.

She kissed him again, desperately pouring all of her feelings into the embrace. At first, he didn't move, but remained an unmoving statue. She rubbed her tongue against his and then sucked on it gently.

Cain pulled away from her and she could feel his stare through the layer of darkness. It was if he was trying to see into her very soul. She opened her mouth to speak when the sound of toenails skittering across a floor caught her attention. A soft woof filled the air before a cold, wet nose thrust itself in her hand.

Katie jumped and then laughed, glad the sensual spell was broken. Talk, she reminded herself. They needed to talk. Needing a moment to compose herself, she greeted Gabriel and rubbed his ears and back. In dog heaven, he stretched out on his back and she accommodated him by scrubbing his belly. All the while, she could feel Cain watching her. Waiting.

Finally, he ran out of patience. "Gabriel, kitchen." Gabriel whined, but with one last lick to Katie's hand, he trotted back to the kitchen.

Katie took off her coat and hung it by the door, aware of Cain's presence as never before. Taking a moment to compose herself, she picked her purse off the floor and hung it next to her coat.

"You seem nervous, Katie. Why?" He walked towards the living room, not glancing behind to see if she was following him. She trailed behind him, determined to get him to talk to her.

It was now or never. "Why didn't you tell me you were E. S. Investors?" Katie waited for him to explain that he was afraid it would have hurt their relationship or that he hadn't wanted to hurt her. She waited. And waited. She anticipated every response except the one she got.

"It was none of your business." Cain's voice was calm and cool as he stood by the fireplace and waited for her reply.

Katie was shocked to her very core. Then she got angry.

"Not my business." She stalked up to him and poked him in the chest with her finger. "Not my business," she repeated. "It was my workplace you were affecting and you knew it because I told you all about it. And worse, you let me and didn't say a thing."

Cain turned and walked to the corner of the room. Bottles clinked and then the sound of liquid being poured into a glass followed. He returned to her side with two glasses filled with an amber liquid. The smell of scotch wafted up to her nose as he pressed one of the glasses into her hands.

"Drink up." He took a sip from his own glass before continuing. "There's no need for this dramatic scene. It simply isn't any of your business."

"How can you say that? I thought we were building something special." She could feel the tears welling in her eyes and her throat tightened as she did her best to fight them back. She had promised herself she wouldn't cry.

"Just because we're sleeping together doesn't mean I'll let you dictate my business practices. It made good sense to buy the building, so I did. End of story." He sounded bored by the whole subject.

"I don't understand." Katie desperately tried to make out his features in the dark, but he kept to the shadows.

"No, I can see that you don't." He paced towards her like some huge jungle cat on the prowl, his eye glittering in the darkness. "Did you think you could manipulate me with sex? Did you think that professing your love would get me to change my mind?" His voice was cold and mocking. "Better women than you have tried, Katie."

Katie couldn't believe the hurtful things he was saying. "How can you even think anything like that, let alone say it?" She was shocked by the conclusions he had drawn. It had never occurred to her that he might view her actions in such a way.

He reached out and caught her chin between his thumb and forefinger and leaned down close. "Because that is what people do." He spoke slowly and clearly as if instructing a child.

"Not when people love each other, they don't," she quietly responded.

Cain laughed bitterly. "Love. I'll tell you about love." He turned away and began to pace the room. "Do you know where I was?"

"You know that I don't." She remained still, not wanting to distract him.

"My mother, my last living relative finally died and I went home to take care of the legal work." He stopped and turned to glare at her. "Home. What a joke."

"I'm sorry about your mother." She reached her hand out to him and dropped it immediately as she sensed his growing anger.

Cain erupted, flinging his glass against the fireplace. It shattered into hundreds of pieces as it crashed into the stone. Shards flew into the air and Katie jumped back in reflex.

"Sorry…" Cain's voice lowered to a harsh whisper. "Don't be sorry. I'm sure as hell not. My parents beat the hell out of me when I was a kid for no other reason than that they were unhappy, miserable people. They never really wanted a kid and they made that fact known until I got too big for them to hit. Then they got afraid of me as I grew bigger and bigger. And do you know what I did?"

He didn't wait for her to answer, but kept right on talking. "I used that fear to make them let me go live with my mother's father. My grandfather, Elijah Stone, was the only person who ever cared for me. I was eighteen when he died." Anger rolled off him in waves. "I've been on my own since."

Katie backed up as Cain stalked towards her. A bead of sweat ran down her back even as she shivered. Deep down, she knew he wouldn't hurt her, but right now he was a frightening sight. His face was a shadowy mask of rage, contorting his features. She'd forgotten how large a man he truly was until he began bearing down on her. His massive chest heaved with every harsh breath he took, and his hands were clenched into giant fists.

"Love. My parents claimed they loved me even as they did everything to destroy me. Love doesn't exist." Cain loomed over her as he finished his tirade. He raked both hands through his hair in agitation. "So you can see, Katie. I can't be controlled or manipulated by anyone or anything. I do as I choose."

Katie tried to stop herself, but she could not restrain the tears that fell from her eyes. The images Cain's words conjured broke her heart. She could picture a young, dark-haired boy being abused and knew that far worse damage had been done to his heart. She reached out to him, wanting to do no more than comfort him. "I'm so sorry."

"Don't you dare feel sorry for me." Cain gripped her by the arms and pulled her close to him.

Katie knew Cain would never have told her any of this if his mother's death hadn't ripped open a wound that had never healed. All his old memories and hurts had boiled over and he'd been unable to contain them. If she hadn't demanded to see him tonight, his defenses would have been firmly back in place and she might never have known anything about his mother or his childhood.

"Don't you dare," he muttered between clenched teeth before leaning down and kissing her hard.

Katie could feel the anger and pain in his bruising kiss, so rather than fight him she gave in to him. His lips ground hard against hers and she forced them to soften. Opening her mouth, she invited him in. His tongue thrust into hers and she responded by wrapping her arms around him. Immediately, his kiss softened. He gently sucked her tongue before licking her swollen lips in silent apology.

When his lips licked up a salty tear, he used his thumbs to carefully wipe her tears away. He took a deep breath before slowly releasing it. "I didn't mean to frighten you."

Katie sniffed back her tears and, although she knew she shouldn't ask, her heart needed to know. "Is that what happened to you?" She brushed the side of his scarred face before he could withdraw.

He quickly captured her hand and drew it back to his lips for a kiss. "No. That was an apartment fire when I was in college." Cain wrapped his arms around her and they held on tight to one another, two people spent by the outpouring of emotions. The dark was like a protective cocoon, protecting them from the rest of the world. Katie took these few moments to try and digest everything she'd just learned about Cain. She sensed his growing restlessness and knew their moment of respite was coming to an end.

Cain pulled back from her embrace, drawing his protective armor back on as he went. Spreading his legs apart, he braced himself as if for a blow. "So where does that leave us?"

"I don't know," she honestly replied.

Cain laughed and it was a hollow sound. "So much for loving me." His voice was laced with sarcasm as he poured himself another drink, gave her a mock salute, and took a large swallow.

"That's not fair." Katie's thoughts were totally disjointed, but she suspected that Cain didn't know what love really was. If his childhood was as bleak as he'd painted it, and she suspected it was even worse, then it was up to her to teach him about true love. Having made her decision, her next action was easier than she expected.

Padding silently across the floor to Cain, she found his hand and gripped it in both of hers. Without saying a word, she tugged at his fingers, urging him to follow her. She knew she couldn't move him without his cooperation, but she needn't have worried, for he put down his glass and followed her unquestioningly.

Katie gingerly picked her way up the darkened hallway and into Cain's bedroom. He stopped right inside the door and wouldn't budge. Instead, he tugged her around to face him.

"There's no going back, you know."

"There never was." Reaching up to him, she tugged his head down to hers and kissed him, holding nothing back. She poured all her pent-up feelings and emotions into this one kiss. Love, tenderness, and passion all mixed together in this heady embrace. Katie gentled him with her hands, massaging his scalp with her fingers before moving downward to rub the tense muscles in his back and his shoulders.

"Damn it, Katie." Cain groaned and pulled her into his embrace as he crushed her mouth against his. Katie was only dimly aware that her feet were dangling in the air above the carpet. She didn't care. She was where she wanted to be. In Cain's embrace.

Chapter Eleven

Cain couldn't believe that Katie was here in his arms. After the explosive scene in the living room, he expected her to run out of his apartment as fast as she could. Again, she had surprised him and run to him, instead of away from him. She felt so damned good in his arms. Too good. He didn't believe in love, but he was no fool. He'd take whatever she would give him and then some.

With Katie still wrapped tight in his arms, he walked towards the bed. She smelled delicious, like vanilla and sunshine. He wanted to devour her from head to toe and everywhere in between. Katie was certainly not the most beautiful woman he'd ever slept with, but there was something about her that rocked him to his very soul. In some intangible way, she completed him.

Right now, she was wiggling in his arms, silently demanding he put her down. Reluctantly, he slid her down the front of his body until her feet touched the floor.

"Let me love you." She pulled his head down and punctuated her words with little kisses. Not waiting for a reply, she pulled back and tugged her sweater over her head and let it drop to the floor. Her bra was next. The slight beam of moonlight bathed her in its glow, making her appear more ethereal than ever. She was a fantasy come to life. But this fantasy was not waiting for him to take control.

While he watched, she toed off her shoes and shimmied out of her jeans and underwear. He stood there riveted by her luminescent skin and her siren's smile. She stood naked and proud before him, allowing his intimate inspection.

Her feet were spread slightly apart, but her toes curled into the rug, as if looking for support. Legs, long and lithe, led to her flat stomach and small waist. Skimming his eye higher, he admired her breasts. Though small, they were perfectly shaped, and the tips were puckered into tight little nubs. The curve of her shoulder flowed up her neck to her face. He knew her face would haunt his dreams for the rest of his life. Her hair stood in spikes, as it usually did, making her look strangely vulnerable. Her eyes glowed with desire and her luscious lips looked slightly swollen from their passionate kisses.

Finally out of patience, she huffed out a deep breath before stepping over to stand in front of him. Reaching out, she began unbuttoning his shirt.

He lifted his hands to stop her, but her low plea of "let me" made him drop them back to his sides. His fists clenched as she worked the buttons open from top to bottom. She pushed open his shirt and rubbed her nose against his chest, breathing deeply.

"You smell good." She kissed her way up his chest. "Warm and sexy." Her tongue flicked out and licked at one of his flat brown nipples. His whole body tightened in response and his hand lifted to cup the back of her head, encouraging her to continue. A sultry laugh escaped her as she kissed her way over to the other side and teased the other nipple.

"You like that as much as I do." Pleased with herself, she continued teasing him. It was a novel experience for a man his stature. Usually both men and women were wary of him because of his immense size, even though he was very careful to control his strength. But Katie, after their initial meeting, had shown no fear at all. In fact, she reached out to him instead of pulling away.

Cain swept one hand over the smooth line of her spine, loving the way she arched under his hand. Tracing the curve of her hip, he finally reached the soft, white globes of her ass. He squeezed them with his palm and urged her closer to him. His cock was hard and he rubbed himself against her stomach.

Her sexy mouth left his chest and she turned her attention to his jeans. Her nimble fingers quickly undid the snap and pulled down the zipper. He clenched his teeth, and his breath came out in a hard hiss as she carefully eased the zipper over his rock-hard erection. Tugging both his jeans and his underwear down over his legs, she then dropped to her knees in front of him and pulled them off one foot and then another, taking his socks and sneakers as she did.

When he was finally naked, except for his shirt, she sat back on her haunches and looked up at him. Taking her time, her gaze slid up his muscular calves, his rock-hard thighs, his huge erection, and his rippling chest, all the way to his face. He knew what he looked like. Huge and rough. His fists clenched at his sides as he waited to see what she would do next.

"You're beautiful," she whispered in awe.

Cain had never been so stunned in his life. Never had anyone said those words to him. All at once, his common sense reasserted itself. She had never seen all of him, he thought sardonically. He was sure she'd have something different to say if she ever saw the extent of his ruined face and scarred body. But still it was nice to hear.

Her palms touched the front of his shins and she slid them up his thighs, coming up on her knees as she did so. Her hands continued their exploration, skimming his waist and stomach as she moved closer to him. Cain could feel his testicles tighten almost painfully as she nuzzled the hair of his groin.

"Katie," he moaned. More than anything, he wanted her to take him in her mouth, but he wouldn't ask. It had to be her choice.

As if she could read his mind, her lips gently skimmed the length of his cock, placing soft kisses from the base to the tip. The ability to think left him. Everything was focused on Katie's mouth and trying to maintain some control. He didn't want to come until he'd had a chance to enjoy her intimate attention.

Katie used her tongue to trace the long blue vein that ran the length of his erection. When she reached the top, she swirled her tongue around the bulbous tip. A small amount of fluid leaked from the tip and she lapped at it before taking the head into her mouth and sucking softly on it. Wrapping one hand around his solid length, she pumped it slowly up and down, while she used her other hand to gently squeeze his testicles.

"Damn it, Katie." His large hands held the back of her head as his hips thrust forward. He felt as if he would explode any moment.

"Don't you like it?" she teased as she licked the tip again before taking him even deeper into his mouth.

"Take more, Katie." He was past all reason now. Having Katie kneeling before him, eagerly taking his cock into her mouth, was better than any fantasy he'd had.

Katie took as much of him into her mouth as she could. Wrapping her lips around him, she gently slid his length in and out of her mouth. The hand at the base of his cock squeezed him tight. That and the sensation of her moist, warm mouth surrounding him had his cock flexing in her mouth.

She made little humming sounds of pleasure as she worked and the vibrations from them almost finished him. It was beyond incredible. Just when he thought he couldn't take any more of her erotic torture, one of her hands began to gently squeeze and play with his testicles.

He hoped she was damn well ready because he couldn't wait any longer. He wanted to come inside her body with her long, luscious legs wrapped tight around him. He wanted to ride her until they both begged for mercy. Cain stepped back from her and his cock came out of her mouth with a little popping sound. She made a little sound of disappointment and reached for him again. Bending down, he pulled her into his arms and then tossed her lightly onto the bed and followed her down to the mattress.

Katie propped herself up on her arms and peppered his face with kisses. Common sense reared its head and he swore. "Damn it. Condom. I need a condom, Katie." He kissed her deeply, thrusting his tongue into her mouth to plunder it.

Everything. He wanted everything. In a monumental feat of restraint, he rolled over and hauled open the drawer of the bedside table. In record time, he was sheathed in a condom.

Rolling back on top of her, he didn't pause, but drove himself deep inside and seated himself to the hilt. Katie was wet and warm and her body welcomed him even as her inner muscles clamped around him.

There was no more time for foreplay. "Wrap your legs around me." Katie immediately wrapped her legs around his waist and locked her ankles together behind his back, pulling him even deeper inside. Cain's forehead dropped to the pillow next to hers as he gasped for breath and control.

But Katie was having none of it. She reared up and used her legs to pull him even closer. Cain was lost. He plunged into her soft, willing body over and over, even as he peppered her face and neck with hot, openmouthed kisses. Their voices mixed together in a symphony of moans and pleas. Gripping her hips in both his hands, he ground his pelvis against her clit, heightening her pleasure. She was completely out of control and so was he, as they both reached for climax.

Katie's inner muscles flexed around his dick and he could feel her coming. Her scream of release was the catalyst for his own. His balls tightened and his hot semen spurted into her until he felt totally empty, yet replete.

In the moment that Katie came, just before him, he heard her voice clearly. "I love you. I love you." It was both a plea and a promise.

Cain slumped over her, unable to form a complete thought, he was so drained. He was in such a stupor, at first he didn't register the fact that one of Katie's hands had slipped inside his shirt and was caressing his scarred shoulder. He pulled out of her and went as still as stone, afraid to move.

Katie ignored the stiffening of his body and continued to trace the irregular ridges of his scars from his shoulder and down his back. Under cover of darkness, she outlined the marks on his left arm and up the front of his chest. She continued until she had mapped out all the scars on his body.

The fabric of his shirt was carefully pushed back, but he didn't move and Katie could only uncover his shoulder. Sighing, she reached up and kissed the areas she could reach. He closed his eyes as the sensation shot through his body. It was almost painful to feel Katie's soft lips against his ravaged flesh.

Settling herself back on the pillows in a comfortable position, Katie tucked the covers around her before she finally spoke. "Why do you hide yourself from me?"

"It's easier that way." The words were out of his mouth before he could stop them.

"Easier for whom? Me or you?" Katie asked him the question that no other had ever dared.

"What is this, a pity fuck?" He heard her soft gasp and for some reason that made him even angrier. "Well, you've done your good deed. You can go if you want or you can stay and fuck some more."

Cain rolled from the bed and went to the bathroom to give himself time to think. By the time he returned to the bedroom, he had his emotions ruthlessly restrained.

He climbed back into bed and pulled Katie into his arms. She surprised him when she rolled easily into his embrace and rested her head on his chest. In truth, he'd expected to find her gone. Instead, her fingers played with the soft line of hair that ran down the center of his stomach and fanned out at his groin. Already, he could feel himself getting aroused again.

"Why didn't you tell me about your business?" Her fingers continued to play up and down his stomach, even as her lips kissed his chest.

"It didn't concern you." He'd made his position clear. It was up to her how she reacted. The subject was closed as far as he was concerned. Right now, the biggest thought on his mind losing himself in Katie's warm, welcoming body.

She sighed deeply and propped herself up on one arm so she was looking down at him. "You didn't trust me."

Her hands reached out to brush the hair off his face, but he grabbed her hand and stopped her. "Katie, just drop it, okay. It doesn't have anything to do with us."

"But I want you to understand my side of things."

A cold feeling of dread began to fill Cain where only moments before a warm feeling of pleasure had reigned. "Is that what this was all about?"

"What are you talking about?"

"Your declaration of love. Your big seduction. Were they both designed to get me to change my mind?" A certainty that she had been trying to manipulate him filled him with an icy anger. His voice was cool and clipped as he continued, "You're good in bed, I'll grant you that, but don't think for one moment you'll affect my decision." He continued cruelly, "You're the best lay I've ever had, but business is business." He knew he was saying things he would later regret, but he couldn't stop the poisonous words from pouring out.

Katie stilled beside him and he braced himself for more pleas, possibly tears and as a last resort, another seduction attempt. He wasn't prepared when she erupted in a flurry of movement. One moment the room was in darkness, the next it was filled with bright light. Katie stood next to the bed like some magnificent avenging angel.

She had never been so furious in all her life. Her chest heaved in anger as she glared down at Cain. "How dare you even suggest such a thing!" Her whole body was shaking as she stood there waiting for him to respond.

It was the first time she'd seen him in the light and the part of her that loved him wanted to crawl back in bed with him and kiss the pain from his poor ravaged body. Cain's left eye was covered in a patch and she could see the scars that came from under it and continued down the side of his face. His neck and chest were filled with slight ridges and pale pink scars.

Cain automatically flicked the shirt so that it covered his left side from shoulder to waist, leaving the right side bare. He turned from her so she was left looking at the right side of his face. Still, in the light, he couldn't hide himself from her. She sensed his discomfort and felt empathy for all the pain he'd suffered, but his scars really weren't as bad as he'd led her to believe.

Instead, her gaze was drawn to the huge expanse of his chest and the gigantic width of his biceps even when he was at rest. The ridges of his flat stomach tapered down to his groin where his erection was growing even as she spoke. It was even more impressive than she'd thought.

Shaking her head, she forced her gaze back to his face. His piercing green eye watched her suspiciously and his jaw was clenched in anger. Well, too bad for him. She was angry too.

Taking his time, he stacked his hands behind his head and then shrugged, allowing the shirt to gape open. "What was I supposed to think?"

"Maybe that I wanted you to share part of your life with me." She stamped her foot in anger. It was either that or smack his gorgeous face. "I didn't for one minute think I could get you to change your mind, but I had hoped you would at least listen to my opinion or explain your reasons for keeping it all a big secret from me."

"It's business, Katie." Cain repeated.

Katie bowed her head in defeat, shaking it slowly in frustration. Unless he was willing to share himself with her, they had no chance at a relationship. They made quite a pair, she exposing her raw emotions and him revealing his physical vulnerability. She laughed and it was a bitter sound. "That's a better explanation than accusing me of whoring myself."

Cain bolted upright in bed and glared at her. He was so upset, he made no effort to keep his face hidden. With his long black hair flowing over one side his face all the way to his shoulders, and the black eye patch covering his eye, he looked like an enraged pirate king. "I never said that."

"Yes, you did," she quietly replied not flinching from the intensity of his green-eyed glare. "When you implied that my declaration of love and my lovemaking were nothing more than a crude attempt to make you change your mind."

"You're twisting my words." Cain reached out to her, but she backed away. If he got her back in bed again, she'd forget her resolve. She had too much respect for herself to allow that to happen.

"No, I think I finally do understand." Gathering her clothes, she quietly padded to the bathroom, where she shut herself inside and quickly pulled on her clothes. At any other time, she would have enjoyed trying out the gigantic tub. It was big enough for two. Squeezing her eyes shut on that painful thought, she counted to ten.

Promising herself she wouldn't cry, she pulled herself together. She straightened her sweater and then wrapped her arms around herself for comfort. The mirror reflected a pale face that looked slightly haggard. Flicking on the cold water tap, she splashed some on her cheeks. She scrubbed her face dry on a towel and ran her fingers through her hair. Satisfied that she looked as good as possible, she was now ready to leave. There was really nothing else she could do.

Cain was still in bed when she left the confines of the bathroom. The room was once again shrouded in darkness, but she could sense his impatience with her.

"There's no need for all this drama. Come here, Katie," he cajoled. When she shook her head, his voice grew hard. "I thought you said you loved me."

Katie bit her lip in pain at the scorn in his tone. "I do love you. The problem is you don't seem to have a care for me at all beyond the confines of your bed."

"Go then. I'm done with you." Anger and pain radiated from his voice.

Katie walked to the doorway, but turned at the last moment. Because she loved him, she owed him one more thing. "You don't need to hide yourself in the dark. You're not as scarred as you think you are." She continued wistfully, "In fact, I think you're quite handsome in a dark, brooding way. Not classically beautiful, but strong and interesting." She shrugged. "That's my opinion, whatever it's worth to you."

"Katie," his voice called to her from the bedroom, but it was too late. Ruthlessly, she ignored the pain in his voice. She couldn't allow him to stop her now when she was feeling weak.

Grabbing her coat, she slammed the door open and raced for the elevator. Luck was with her and the door opened as soon as she pressed the button. Quickly, she stepped in and stabbed the down button. The door was closing when she heard the sound of footsteps following her.

Katie burst from the elevator, raced across the garage and quickly left the building. Hurrying down the road, she dashed the tears from her eyes, all the while telling herself it was just the wind making them water. It was a frigid night and Katie felt so cold from the inside out.

A light from an all-night diner beckoned her, and she slipped inside, thankful for its warmth. The bell over the door jangled as she entered. She noted that the place was empty, except for two men sipping coffee at the counter and chatting to the waitress. No one paid any attention to her, for which she was grateful.

A payphone was tucked just inside the door and Katie sighed with relief. Reaching for her purse, or where it was supposed to be, she closed her eyes on a wave of despair. It was still hanging up by Cain's front door, and there was no way she was going back for it.

Digging in her pocket for loose change, she decided she didn't have any choice but to call Lucas to come pick her up. She closed her eyes as a wave of despair washed over her, she really wasn't up to his interrogation right now. It was taking all of her energy not to burst into tears. Her hand brushed something as she searched for a spare quarter for a call and she pulled out the small square of cardboard Quentin had given her.

Clutching it like a lifeline, she dialed the number quickly before she talked herself out of it. She hoped he'd meant what he'd said.

"Quentin." The voice was clipped.

Katie swallowed hard around the lump in her throat. "James…"

"Katie, is that you?" The voice was more concerned now. Warm and caring.

Tears flowed freely down her face. "I'm sorry to bother you." She sniffed and scrubbed at her tears.

"Where are you?" She could hear the rustling sound of clothes being pulled on as he spoke.

"I'm at a diner just down the road from Cain's. I left my purse at his place and I'm so cold, James."

She could hear the worry in his voice as he spoke. "Give me the number of the phone you're calling from." He wrote down the number as she read it off the phone. "Hang up and I'll call you back on my cell phone."

Reluctantly, she replaced the receiver and a few seconds later it rang and she grabbed it on the first ring. Quentin kept her on the line talking until he pulled up in front of the diner. Hurrying inside, he pried the phone from her hand and hung it up. Bustling her into the car, he drove her home, watching her worriedly, but not asking any questions.

He helped Katie out of the car when they reached her apartment and he walked her up the stairs. Katie was grateful that she carried her keys in her coat pocket and not her purse, or she would have had no choice but to call Lucas to get his spare one. When she unlocked the door she turned to face James.

"Thank you." She didn't know what else to say. She really looked at him for the first time since he'd picked her up at the diner and realized that his coat wasn't buttoned properly and his hair was all standing on end. He'd literally hauled himself out of bed and run to help her.

He just gave her a sad smile and patted her on the arm. "Anything I can do to help..." He trailed off. "If you want to talk any time, I'm a good listener."

Katie stood on her toes and kissed his cheek and was surprised when he colored. "You're a good friend." She turned and entered her apartment. Giving him one last wave as she closed the door, she stopped when he started to speak again.

"Don't give up on him, Katie." There was a plea in his voice.

"It's the other way around. He's given up on me." With that, she closed the door and locked it. Leaning against it, she waited until his footsteps faded and she knew she was alone.

Stumbling down the hall, she pulled off her clothes and pulled on her warmest nightgown and a thick pair of socks before falling into bed. Pulling all the blankets over her, and tucking them in tight, she longed for the forgetfulness of sleep.

The phone rang shrilly next to the bed and she stared at it, afraid to move. It continued to ring and she counted them all the way to fifteen before they finally stopped. Reaching over she pulled the plug out of the phone and let it drop to the floor. Tunneling under the covers once again, she reached for, and finally found, peace as sleep overtook her.

Chapter Twelve

Katie lay in bed and stared at the wall. It seemed wrong somehow that the sun was shining bright outside. She could hear the sounds of traffic as people started their day. The truth of the matter was that, even when your heart was broken, life did indeed go on whether you wanted it to or not. Katie wanted to stay in bed, but she really needed to go to the bathroom.

Throwing back the covers, she stumbled across the hall and made quick use of the facilities. After washing her hands, she scrubbed her face with cold water and brushed her teeth. Feeling marginally better, she ran a brush through her hair and sized herself up in the mirror over the sink. Her eyes were bloodshot and she looked a little pale, but other than that, she looked normal. Somehow, she'd expected her inner turmoil to be reflected on her face, but surprisingly enough, she looked the same as she always did.

Back in her bedroom, she pulled off her sleepwear and dressed in a comfortable pair of sweatpants and a favorite pullover. Comfort was the order of the day. She tossed the covers over the bed, but didn't bother to make it properly. There was no point, as she'd probably be crawling back into it later for a nap.

She wasn't hungry, but she was incredibly thirsty. A glass of cold orange juice was exactly what she needed. Padding to the kitchen on stocking feet, she poured herself a glass of juice and drank it down in one long gulp. Filling the glass again, she tossed the empty container in her recycle bin, picked up her glass, and shuffled into the living room and plopped down on the sofa.

Katie knew she was purposely avoiding all thought of Cain. The last few days had been an emotional roller coaster and right now all she wanted was peace. Tipping her head back to rest on the back of the sofa, she closed her eyes and held the glass in her two hands.

She tried to relax, but she remained tense. The paintings lined up against the wall were haunting her with their images of Cain. Cain as an illusive shadow, an image in the dark, and finally, in the last one, reaching into the light. The empty canvas on her easel was calling to her for completion.

Opening her eyes, she allowed them to gently graze over the finished paintings. Cain's aloneness was evident in the pictures. He was like some wild animal that longed for comfort, but snapped and snarled at anyone who dared to approach. She swallowed the lump in her throat. Somehow, in spite of his secretive ways, he had slipped past her defenses and into her heart. She sensed that here was a kindred spirit with even more barriers than herself. But it was now obvious that she wasn't the right woman to break down his walls, to reach the man beneath.

Katie took another sip of juice and enjoyed the sensation as the cold, tangy liquid glided down her throat. Resolutely, she plunked the glass on the coffee table, came to her feet, and approached the blank canvas.

Readjusting the easel to catch the best light, she picked up a pencil and began to sketch. As she worked, she got faster and faster until she had the basic shape of the picture she wanted to paint. Standing back, she looked it over carefully. Satisfied, she began to pick and choose colors, squirting them onto her palate. Then, selecting a brush, she began to paint.

As it always did, time lost all meaning as she painted. Her art had always been her way of expressing herself and now she needed that release more than she ever had in her entire life. Every emotion, every feeling, every tear shed, was poured into the creation of her latest work.

She was placing the final brushstrokes when a pounding on her front door disturbed her. Startled, her hand jerked and she stared critically at her work to make sure that she hadn't smeared any paint. Ignoring the continued pounding on the front door, she laid down her brush and stepped back from the easel to get a better perspective on the canvas. It was all there in front of her. She felt open and vulnerable, but in some way she felt a little bit better. The painting had been cathartic, a way of purging the worst of the pain and sorrow.

The sound of a key turning in her lock finally broke the spell the picture had cast upon her. She hurried to the door and reached it just as it swung open. Lucas stepped inside, his face set in hard, angry lines. Closing the door behind him, he crossed his arms over his chest and glared at her.

"Where the hell have you been?" He stood there as unmoving as a mountain, and his solid presence reassured her as nothing else could.

Katie leaned up and kissed him on the cheek. "I'm sorry I worried you."

"Worry." Lucas unlocked his arms and ran his fingers through his hair and took a deep breath. "Katie, I've been calling all day long. It's almost dinnertime and you promised you'd call me. Why didn't you answer your damn phone?"

"Oh, I'm so sorry. I unplugged it last night after I got home and I was working today and forgot to plug it back in…" she trailed off as his attention was drawn from her to the easel in the corner.

Slowly, he walked to the other side of the room. He stood there with his hands on his hips and just stared at her painting. Then he looked at the other three finished works and then back to her latest one. He said nothing for the longest time and she began to fidget.

"You love him, don't you?" It was more a statement than a question, but she answered him anyway.

"Yes, I do." Going over to join him, she wrapped one arm around his waist and he automatically adjusted his body so that she was sheltered under his arm. "But he's not ready to love anyone. He may never be ready."

"I'm sorry, Katie." His voice was low, the sentiment heartfelt.

"Me too." She took a deep breath before continuing. "But life goes on and I don't regret one minute I spent with him. He brought me back to life when I hadn't even realized I'd been sleepwalking through my own life. For that fact alone, I'll always love him."

"Is there anything I can do?"

Katie looked at the four paintings and came to a decision. "I left my purse at Cain's home last night when I…left. Would you go and get it for me? I'm not ready to see him right now."

Lucas gave her a reassuring squeeze before releasing her. "Sure, honey, I'll go right now. What's the address?" He was already starting for the door as he spoke.

"Lucas." The soft plea in her voice stopped him. "Will you do something else for me?"

He braced himself as if he knew her request was something he wasn't particularly going to enjoy. "Yeah."

"Will you take these paintings to him?" Katie licked her dry lips. "Tell him...tell him that they're a gift from me."

Lucas hung his head for a moment, fighting all his protective instincts. But in the end, he replied, as she knew he would. "If that's what you want."

"Thank you, Lucas."

"Only for you, Katie. I don't think the bastard deserves them." Lucas glared at the paintings. "They're the best work you've ever done, but if you want him to have them, and there's nothing I can do to stop you..." He waited as she shook her head, no. "Then I'll make sure he gets them."

Katie nodded and then carefully began to wrap the paintings for transport, taking special care with the newest one, which was still very wet. It would take months for the paintings to dry properly, but they could do that at Cain's home. Lucas carried the first three while she followed him down to his car, carefully carrying the latest one. When the other three were stowed properly, Lucas took the newest one from her and laid it carefully on top.

"I'll be back as soon as I deliver these and get your purse." He leaned down and kissed her on the forehead. "You go on up and rest. I'll stop and pick up a pizza on my way back."

For a moment, Katie gave in to her despair and clung to Lucas in a desperate hug, not wanting him to leave her.

He returned her embrace and waited patiently for her to release him. "I love you, Lucas."

"Me too, Katie." Lucas climbed into his car and waited as she gave him the address. He started the vehicle, but waited until she was back inside the building before he drove away.

The steady buzzing at his door was getting irritating. Whoever was there wasn't going to go away, at least not without dire threats. Gabriel began to bark, so Cain heaved himself out of his comfortable chair in his study and walked towards the intercom.

He didn't want to leave the painting. It was the only connection he had with Katie. She'd run out so quickly last night and wasn't answering his calls. He wouldn't have slept at all last night, except Quentin had called him and assured him that he'd seen Katie safely home. The displeasure in Quentin's voice had been obvious last night. Cain had quietly thanked him and hung up on him.

As he neared the front door, he noticed something he had missed last night when he'd chased after Katie. Her purse was hanging from a hook on the coat rack by the front door. For a moment, his hopes grew. Maybe it was Katie at the door coming to get her wallet. He hurried to the intercom, hushing Gabriel as he went.

"Katie," he barked into the intercom. Silence greeted him and then a very irritated male voice answered him.

"No, it's not Katie. I'm here to pick up Katie's purse and to drop off something to you. So open the damn door." His voice was openly hostile.

Cain felt his own anger rising. "Who the hell are you?"

"Lucas Squires," he replied shortly.

This was the man that Katie worked for. The one she was close to, and if Cain was honest with himself, the one he was jealous of. He pressed down on the security button, unlocking the outer door. "Come on in. Take the elevator at the far end to the top."

There was no reply, but Cain hadn't really expected one. He opened the door and waited impatiently until the elevator began to rise. The door finally opened and the man who stepped out was not quite what he expected. This guy ran a coffee shop, but he was built like a linebacker. He carefully removed four large packages from the elevator, one at a time, and propped them against the wall of the small hallway. He picked up one and effortlessly carried it in his massive arms. Lucas might have been shorter than him, but he was built like a solid brick wall and looked as tough as nails. And right now the look in his eyes said that he'd gladly take a swing at him if given half a chance.

Cain sighed and stepped back, holding the door open. "You might as well come in."

"I don't plan on staying long," came the sardonic reply.

"How is she?" Cain asked before he could stop himself.

Lucas carefully laid the package down before facing Cain. He placed his hands on his hips and just glared at him. "Why do you care? And why the hell is it so dark here? Be a man and show yourself."

Cain reacted to that taunt immediately. He flicked on a light, pulled himself up to his full height and flexed his fingers into fists. If Lucas wanted a fight, he was more than willing to oblige.

Lucas looked unimpressed and repeated his question. "Why do you care?" This time his voice was low and taunting.

Cain was surprised and pleased that Lucas wasn't intimidated by him. In some perverse way, he was glad that Katie had a strong protector. "I do care."

Lucas just shook his head in disgust. "Katie will be fine. She's a strong lady." Turning away, he went back into the hallway and got the next package. When they were all inside the apartment, he began to unwrap the canvases. "You don't deserve her. You're obviously not good enough for her."

Cain's reply was stark. "I know."

"Well, for some reason Katie saw fit to love you, but there's no accounting for taste." Lucas continued his work.

Cain winced as the other man spoke bluntly. "You don't mince words, do you?"

"Nope. Especially not when you were idiot enough to throw away the love of a good woman like Katie." Lucas stopped his task for a moment and stood facing Cain. "Look, I don't know you, but I do know Katie. She would never try to manipulate you or use you in any way. That's not her style. Katie doesn't play games. But she was devastated that you'd kept secrets from her." Lucas stared hard at Cain as he finished. "From what I can see, you're the one playing games with her."

Cain had no defense against his words and said nothing as Lucas began lining up four paintings against the wall, one after another. He recognized Katie's work immediately and was shocked to discover that he was the subject of all of them. A hiss of pain escaped him as he studied each of them in turn.

Lucas stood back, satisfied with his work. "Where's her purse?"

Cain indicated the coat rack by the front door, but he couldn't take his eyes off the paintings in front of him.

Lucas tucked Katie's purse under his arm and turned to go, satisfied that he had fulfilled his part of the bargain. He glanced back at Cain, who was transfixed by Katie's work. "If you can't see the truth in those paintings, then you really are a fool." On that final note, Lucas quietly left the apartment, leaving Cain to his own thoughts.

When the door closed behind Lucas, Cain fell to his knees in front of the paintings. It was like reading a story of their relationship. From the first one where he was nothing but a shadow in the dark, to the next one where he was partially visible on the street, and to the third one in which he was inviting her to share not only dinner, but his dark world with him.

But it was the final painting that moved him the most. He was lying in bed, but he was fully in the light. Katie had been brutally honest in her depiction of him. The patch on his eye, the scars on his face, neck, arm, and chest were all visible, but she had captured much more than that. Even at rest, the strength in his body, his sheer size was evident. The silky strands of his black hair were pushed back from his face. The gleam in his green eye was filled with male satisfaction as he held one hand out, beckoning to an unseen woman. The crisp white sheets next to him were rumpled, indicating that the woman had just risen and he was trying to entice her back to bed.

Then he noticed that the woman was in darkness. Katie had painted herself as a shadow fading into the darkness. She was succumbing to his darkness as she tried to guide him into her light, her love. How long he sat there and stared at the painting he didn't know. It was only when Gabriel licked his face and whined that Cain discovered his cheek was wet. He hadn't cried since he was a child.

Katie had painted a masterpiece of love. She was willing to let him go if he could not accept her love. No blame. No recriminations. All he sensed was a sadness that he was unable to reach out and take the love offered him.

He was a bloody fool. He had thought he was so clever, hiding himself from her. Thinking that she would not be able to accept him as he was. In truth, Lucas was right, he was a coward and an idiot. In seeking to protect himself, he had thrown away the very things he had been looking for all of his life—love and acceptance.

He may very well be a fool, but he also learned from his mistakes. Katie had met him more than halfway and now it was his turn to reach out to her if he had a chance of saving their relationship. He was gambling on the fact that she truly seemed to love him and he was ruthless enough to exploit that fact if it meant getting her back in his life.

Pushing himself to his feet, he took a moment to scratch Gabriel's head and ear to reassure the dog that everything was all right. Gabriel continued to hover close to him, following him up and down the hallway as he moved the paintings.

Carefully, Cain carried one painting at a time until they were all leaning against the wall in the study. He eased himself into his chair and began to mull over ideas.

Gabriel flopped on the floor next to his feet and kept one canine eye on him for a long time before finally going to sleep.

It was late when he finally left the study and crawled into bed. He had made up his mind about what he had to do. It had to work. The alternative, a life without Katie, was no longer acceptable.

Chapter Thirteen

Katie refilled the sugar dispenser and then added napkins to the holder before wiping down the table. She moved to the next table by rote and began the routine all over again. Glancing at the clock, she breathed a sigh of relief. It was ten minutes to closing. She finished the last table and took a quick look around, pleased when she saw only a single couple at a table in the corner. They had already paid for their order and looked as if they were almost finished their coffee.

Her mind drifted back to this past weekend, which had passed in a blur of emotion. It was hard to believe that only a few days ago, she was happily going about her life and anticipating spending a weekend with Cain. Instead, the last week had been an emotional roller coaster.

Lucas had plied her with pizza and two comedy videos he picked up on his way back to her place Saturday night. Katie couldn't even remember what the movies were. She was just glad for his company. She didn't know what had transpired between him and Cain. He hadn't said anything and she hadn't asked.

Lucas had shown up again early on Sunday morning and dragged her out to breakfast, insisting that she join him for pancakes and syrup. They followed breakfast with a long drive, stopping occasionally to shop at an indoor flea market, a thrift shop, and finally a bookstore. An early dinner had capped off the day and the sun had gone down for the day by the time Lucas had taken her home. She loved him for keeping her company and trying to take her mind off of her problems.

Scooting behind the counter, Katie emptied the last of the trays from the display case. Carefully, she transferred the remaining cookies and treats to a large plastic container. They would be bagged and reduced for a quick sale to the morning crowd. Before closing the container, she selected two cinnamon rolls and put them in a takeout box. She approached the couple in the corner with a forced smile on her face.

"We're closing now, but I brought you a couple of cinnamon buns for the road." Katie had long ago found that you could get rid of customers at closing if you offered them a free treat. She didn't resort to this tactic very often, but today she was desperate to just go home.

As expected, the couple gratefully accepted her offering, tugged on their jackets and wished her well as they headed out the door. Katie called her goodbyes as they left, but was already ducked behind the counter, grabbing the closed sign from underneath. Katie shrieked as something cold hit her hand. Jumping back she hit her hip on the counter and cursed.

Sitting before her, totally unconcerned, was Gabriel. His tail was wagging, and in his mouth he carried a single red rose with a note attached. Her hand automatically reached out to pet him even as her eyes searched for Cain, but he was nowhere to be seen.

"Why am I not surprised?" she muttered to the dog. Still, she could not resist the flower and carefully took it from the dog's mouth. Gabriel licked her hand as she did so, happy that he had discharged his duty.

Lucas stepped out from the back. "Are we closed?"

"Almost." She smiled at the dog who was still wagging his tail happily. "We had a last-minute customer."

Lucas scowled and glanced around the room. His gaze lit on the rose in Katie's hand and the attached note. "Well, are you going to read it?"

"I'm almost afraid to," she answered honestly.

Lucas's eyes softened. "Do you want me to read it for you?"

"No, I'll do it." Taking her time, she removed the note from the envelope. It was simple and to the point. She read it aloud. "If you can find it in your heart to talk to me, I'll be waiting." It was not signed.

"What are you going to do?" Lucas's voice was soft behind her.

"I honestly don't know." Katie felt so conflicted. Part of her wanted to race outside to find him, while another part wanted to run home and hide. But she had never been a coward and didn't know if she could live with herself if she didn't at least hear what he had to say.

"Yes, you do know." Lucas came up behind her and placed both of his large hands on her shoulders and gave her a reassuring squeeze.

She reached up and touched one of his hands, silently acknowledging his comfort. "I hate it when you're right." Sighing, she stepped away and pulled off her apron.

Lucas gave her a little push towards the back. "Go get your coat on and I'll finish closing."

When she returned a few moments later with her coat and purse, Lucas had the storefront closed, the lights turned off, and the cash pulled from the register. The shop was dark, as the sun had already gone down, and the only light was the soft glow of the security lights. She walked over to him and he pulled her into his arms.

As he hugged her, he reached down to whisper in her ear. "One chance, Katie. But, if he hurts you again, I'll beat him up for you."

Katie laughed, as he'd known she would. "Thanks. You're a good friend."

"I know." He released her and gave her a rare smile. "Call me if you need me."

"Promise." Pulling her purse securely over her shoulder, she headed towards the door where Gabriel was patiently waiting.

The moment she opened the door, Gabriel shot out of the shop and to the curb where his limo was waiting. Quentin was standing there, holding the door open, with a slight enigmatic smile on his face. Gabriel barked impatiently from the interior of the vehicle. Katie hesitated. She'd been expecting Cain.

"He's waiting at home for you." Quentin answered her unasked question. "I was to take you to your place if you didn't want to see him. The choice is yours."

Katie gave him a sad smile. "We both know I'm going." She climbed into the back of the limo and rested her head on the back of the plush seat. Her head pounded, she was so tired. She'd hardly slept at all the last couple nights and was exhausted. It had taken everything she'd had today just to function properly and smile occasionally at the customers.

Gabriel placed his head on her lap and whined softly. "It's all right," she comforted him as she petted him. Closing her eyes, she tried to relax and not think about what Cain had to say. She'd thought they'd said it all the other night.

All too soon the car came to a stop. Before she could gather herself to open the door, Quentin was there. Grateful for his support, she took the hand he offered and climbed from the backseat. "Thank you, James," she murmured.

"Just go right up," he told her as he led her to the familiar steel door at the back of the stately, stone building and opened it. He nudged her elbow when she stood staring at the opening.

Katie forced her tired body to move across the private parking garage to the elevator. She was aware of Gabriel padding along next to her and of the outer door closing behind her. The sound of the limo driving away made her feel lonely even though Gabriel was next to her. James at least was an ally, Gabriel was Cain's emissary. Not that she could hold that fact against such a sweet dog, but in the end, he was Cain's pet.

She pressed the button to summon the elevator and stepped inside when it arrived. The ride to the top went too quickly. The door slid open and she cautiously stepped out into the hall. The apartment door was open, so she went right inside. "Cain," she called softly as she stepped inside. There was no reply, and no visible sign of him.

Taking her time, she removed her coat and hung both it and her purse on the familiar coat rack. She tugged at her sweater as doubts assailed her. Maybe she should have gone home and changed first. She'd had a long day's work in these clothes, and she felt grimy and sweaty. Gabriel nudged at her leg impatiently.

"What do you want?" Gabriel responded to her voice by trotting down the hall. She reluctantly followed him and it only took her a moment to realize he was leading her to the rooftop garden.

Katie stepped into the familiar garden and looked around. The air was alive with the scent of fresh earth and flowers. The lush foliage made the air slightly humid, but not uncomfortable. It was an oasis in the middle of the frigid, cold winter. Soft music played in the background and mingled with the sound of the water running in the fountain. The table was set, just like the last time, and two glasses of wine had been poured.

Katie sensed she wasn't alone and her gaze immediately went to the far corner. The large shadow in the corner was one she knew intimately. She bowed her head as a wave of sorrow washed over her. He was still hiding from her after everything they'd been through.

"How did you know I was here?" His voice, low and sexy made a shiver run down her spine.

"I could feel you there," she replied honestly.

Cain stepped out from the shadows. He walked straight towards her under the glow of the patio lights, never once trying to keep his face hidden. For the first time, his long dark hair was slicked back from his face and hung down to his shoulders.

Katie couldn't tear her gaze away as he sauntered towards her. His arms hung loosely at his sides, but his hands were fisted and his shoulders were stiff, indicating that he wasn't as relaxed as he was trying to portray. The raw emotion on his face almost made her cry out in pain. He looked ravaged.

Unable to stop herself, Katie took a step backwards. If he put his hands on her, she'd forget all about talking and fall into bed with him. This time, she was determined that they would talk.

Cain came to an abrupt halt in front of her. Anguish filled his eye as he held himself utterly still. Every muscle in his body was clenched tightly. "I guess I deserve that." His voice was filled with pain as he spoke.

Katie relented instantly and reached out to him. Slowly, carefully, he took her hand in his. His grasp was firm and warm as she allowed him to lead her over to the table.

"Please sit."

Katie sat and immediately picked up her wine and took a sip. Her mouth was so dry, she didn't know if she could speak. Cain hovered behind her a moment. She could feel his heat and his uncertainty. Her shoulders tensed as she waited to see what he would do. He lightly touched her head with his hand before easing his body around the table to seat himself across from her.

"I'm sorry I hurt you, Katie," he began abruptly.

"I know." She added nothing more, but waited.

Cain shook his head. "I didn't think you'd make it easy." His mouth quirked up in a half-grin as he teased her.

"Why should I?"

Cain sobered immediately. "You shouldn't." Getting up from the table, Cain began to pace, hands clasped behind his back, as if to keep himself from reaching out and pulling her into his arms.

Katie turned in her seat so she could watch him. He moved like a large jungle cat on the prowl, all sinewy muscle and grace. Darkness emanated from him that, she'd now come to understand, was simply part of his personality. He was like some dark, pagan god come to earth. He would never be an easy man to love, but if he would open himself up to her, she knew his love would be steadfast and forever.

Emotion rolled off him and again the sheer force of his presence struck her. He had no idea just how charismatic and powerful a man he was. Her eyes softened as she watched him gather his thoughts. As if feeling her stare, he stopped pacing and pinned her with his glare.

"I know I can be a hard man to live with."

Laughter fell from Katie's lips. Cain looked so disgruntled at her action that she laughed even harder. He scowled at her for a moment before smiling self-consciously. A moment later, he chuckled. "I guess you already know that."

"I guess I do." Katie managed to contain her laughter, but she couldn't hide her smile. He was trying so hard to explain himself and that had to mean he cared about her. Even as Katie's brain urged her to caution, hope was growing in her heart.

Cain stalked back to the table and went down on one knee in front of her. He cupped her face in his hands and slowly bent his face to hers, brushing his lips softly against hers. Drawing back, he released her face and took both her hands in his.

"I may not know what love is, but I need you like I need air to breathe. You are the light in the darkness of my life and when I drove you away I was in the dark by myself again. I didn't like it. I want to talk to you, hear your laughter, and have you tease me, yell at me, and challenge me. I've never met anyone as genuine and real as you are. Everything about you fascinates me. I need you, Katie. Don't let me go back into the darkness."

Cain sat there at her feet, waiting for her to decide his fate. Never, she thought, had a man loved a woman as much as he loved her. For some reason he didn't know that what he was feeling was love. But she knew and that was enough for her. She took a deep breath to reply and could feel the salt on her lips from the tears that slipped from her eyes. This man in front of her, making himself vulnerable to her, was her man, for better or for worse.

Mistaking her silence for rejection, Cain desperately tried again. "I'll give you the building as a present. Just stay."

Katie tugged her hand away from him and placed it over his mouth stopping him from saying more. She didn't want him humbled and she didn't want him to think he had to buy her love.

"No, Cain."

"Please, Katie," he pleaded.

"I don't want your building or your money." She hurried on before he could speak. "All I want is you." He sat back with a stunned look on his face. Leaning forward, she placed a soft kiss on his ravaged cheek.

He shuddered and buried his face in her lap. His arms banded around her waist, holding her tight. Katie ran her fingers through his hair, silently trying to comfort him. Cain suddenly pulled her from her chair and into his lap. His embrace was so tight that she could barely breathe. Rather than pull away, she wrapped her arms around him and held him close. She could sense the desperation in his actions.

"I knew you'd give me another chance when I saw the paintings," Cain muttered as he began to cover her face in frantic kisses. "I'll make you happy. I promise you."

Katie cupped his face in her hands, forcing him to look at her. "You'll make me happy and sad. Just as I'll do the same to you." He stilled, all his attention focused on her, as he listened to her. "Cain, I don't want you to promise me the impossible. That's too much pressure for any relationship. It's not your responsibility to make me happy. All you have to do is be yourself and share your life with me."

"That's all?" She could feel the muscles in his shoulders relaxing, his whole body practically sighing in relief.

"Yes." She kissed him playfully on the nose. "That's all."

Reaching up, he brushed at the tears on her face. "I'm not really crying," she reassured him.

"I know, honey." He continued to run his thumbs over her cheeks and suddenly a smile lit his face. "But I'd have given you anything. You should have at least asked for a car or a house."

"I already have everything I want," Katie assured him. She wanted him to understand that her love was unconditional and did not depend on gifts given or offered.

"I don't know what I did to deserve you, but I've got you now and I'm keeping you." Cain shifted her so that one arm was under her knees and the other around her shoulders. In an amazing feat of strength, he rose from the floor with her clutched tight in his arms. For a moment, he just stood there in the peace and quiet of the garden, giving her plenty of time to object to his actions.

Katie snuggled into his embrace and wrapped her arms around his neck. Every muscle in Cain's body tensed, and then he swore and spun around. Quickly, he strode from the garden and towards his bedroom, with her clasped safely in his arms. Using his booted heel, he kicked the door shut and moved towards the bed.

He hesitated for a moment before lowering her legs to the floor. When she was steady, he stepped away and turned on a light. It was low, but she could see him perfectly. Eagerly, she stepped towards him.

"Love me, Cain." Her soft plea moved him to action.

Taking his time, he pulled her cotton top over her head and dropped it to the floor. Reaching behind her, he unhooked her bra and slid the straps down her arms. The bra landed on the floor next to her top. His breathing was labored but he made no move to touch her. Instead, he moved on to her jeans. The button was opened and the zipper tugged down and a second later he tugged both her jeans and underwear down to her knees.

Guiding her, he sat her on the side of the bed. One at a time, he pulled off her boots. Leaning forward, he rained kisses down her thighs and calves as he removed her jeans and panties. His breath was hot and moist on her already heated skin and she could feel her whole body clench in response. He noticed her reaction and nuzzled the pubic hair between her legs before sitting back on his haunches to look his fill.

"You are the most beautiful woman I've ever seen." His voice was filled with an honest appreciation for her that made her blush from head to toe. Katie squirmed on the bed, and Cain, sensing her discomfort, pulled back the sheets and urged her under the covers.

Katie got comfortable and settled herself against the softness of the pillows. A quiet contentment filled her as she waited for Cain to join her.

Chapter Fourteen

Cain wanted to pinch himself to make sure he wasn't dreaming. But then, no dream could capture the sheer beauty of Katie as she watched him from the bed. She looked absolutely delectable tucked cozily under the covers. From the moment she'd entered the rooftop garden, he'd been as hard as a rock. Katie turned him on faster than any other woman ever had. Her every look, every smile, was an erotic promise. Hell, the woman only had to breathe and he wanted her.

Bending over, he tugged off his boots and socks. Straightening, he began the slow torturous process of unbuttoning his shirt. He wanted to share himself with her, but a part of him still wanted to hide the ugliness of his scars.

"It's all right, you know." Katie's voice was a soft invitation from the bed. "I've already seen your scars. What you don't seem to understand is that I'm hot for your body." Her hot gaze scorched his already inflamed skin.

A sudden bark of laughter escaped him and he realized just how foolish he was being. Grabbing his shirt, he tugged it over his head and dropped it to the floor. He shucked his jeans and underwear and stood there totally naked and exposed in the soft light.

"Come to bed." The erotic purr was more than he could withstand and he crawled into bed next to her.

Cain really looked into Katie's eyes. She truly wanted him. There was no way she could fake the hungry look in her eyes and the quickening of her breath. Cain took a deep breath. He could smell Katie's arousal, the alluring scent of her skin and the slight sweet smell of vanilla, and he hadn't even touched her yet. That was the reassurance he needed.

Propping himself on one arm, he leaned over her. "You really want me, don't you?" He could hear the surprise in his own voice.

Rather than answer him with words, Katie reached up and wrapped her hand around the back of his neck and tugged him down so she could kiss him. Cain eased down slowly and allowed her to kiss him at her leisure. For once there was no hurry, no dawn deadline. There was all the time in the world to explore.

Katie's lips met his in a soft seeking of pleasure that soon was not enough for either of them. Her tongue moved boldly into his mouth and he answered in kind, sucking on her tongue, licking at her lips. He drank in her sweetness and then went back for more. Her taste, her texture was like drinking the finest wine and eating the richest food. The sensation was incredible. He could feel his testicles tighten at the sheer pleasure of kissing her.

He left her lips and sampled her forehead, her eyes, her cheeks and her chin. There was no part of her that he didn't want to taste. Katie's hands were frantic as she clutched at his shoulders and stroked his back. At one point, she even grabbed his hair to try and lead him back to her mouth.

Cain trapped her hands in his. He'd come too soon if she didn't stop, and this time he was determined to do things right. "Roll over on your stomach for me."

"Cain," she grumbled his name as she tried to pull her hands free from his grip.

He shook his head. "Please."

Katie gave him a disgruntled look, tugged her hands free, and then flopped over onto her stomach. "I hope you're happy, because I'm not."

Cain smiled and was thankful that Katie couldn't see his expression. He was sure she wouldn't appreciate his sense of humor at the moment. "I'll make it worth your while," he whispered fervently in her ear.

Katie buried her face in the pillow, saying nothing. She sighed deeply and tapped her fingers on the pillows next to her head.

Cain chuckled, unable to restrain his happiness. That was his Katie. She was one of the few people who seemed unimpressed by his physical size and disfigurement. Come to think about it, his power and wealth didn't impress her either. Cain grabbed a condom from the bedside table and quickly rolled it on.

When she impatiently tried to turn over in the bed, he quickly bent down and nipped the back of her neck with his teeth. She moaned and slumped back onto the pillows. Consolidating his position, Cain kissed and nipped his way down her spine while his hands grasped the globes of her ass and massaged them.

"You've got the sweetest ass," he muttered as he licked the line between the top of her leg and her behind.

Katie squirmed on the bed, but still he didn't release her. Instead, he plumped each cheek in his hand and took little love bites across her behind. Katie shrieked and bucked but he was relentless in his efforts to pleasure her.

Grabbing the pillow next to her, she flung it backwards at him. Surprised by her action, it hit him square in the face before landing on her back. He flicked the pillow away and leaned over her back, covering her body with his. She tensed as he ran his tongue around the outside of her ear. "Now you're gonna pay."

Katie responded by reaching behind and pinching him. He jerked back. "You little wildcat."

Holding her with one hand pressed into the base of her spine, he slowly ran one finger down the dark cleft of her behind. She arched her bottom towards his hand, trying to deepen his touch, but he continued to tease her with a light touch, not allowing his fingers to explore the hot, needy area between her legs.

"You're a brute," came her muffled complaint.

"You haven't seen anything yet," he promised. He continued to tease and torment her for another moment before flipping her easily in the bed so she lay sprawled on her back.

Katie blinked up at him, her expression a combination of arousal and frustration. Cain linked her fingers with his and wedged his body between her legs. Katie spread her legs wider to accommodate his size. Holding her hands down on the bed, he leaned forward and nuzzled between her breasts.

Ignoring her pleas and moans, he licked at each breast, tasting and teasing them. He kissed her pale, plump flesh but avoided her nipples, which were tight, distended buds, begging to be sucked. Cain held out as long as he could. His cock was screaming to be buried inside her, but he had to taste all of her first.

Taking one of her nipples gently between his teeth, he held it secure while he flicked it with his tongue. Katie squealed and pleaded. She tore her hands from his grasp and used them to anchor his face to her breast while arching herself closer to him. Cain used his free hand to plump her other breast, using his thumb and forefinger to pleasure the pouting nipple. Her hands moved lower to knead the muscles in his back.

Cain pulled his mouth away and blew softly on her moist skin. Moaning, she arched her head back on the pillow. The sting of her nails digging into his back felt so damned good. He'd never seen a woman so naturally responsive or as beautiful in her passion as Katie.

Reluctantly dragging himself away from her breasts, he kissed a line down her smooth, white belly. He nipped at the indention of her waist and sucked on her hipbones. Settling himself between her legs, he separated the folds of sensitive skin and breathed in her sweet, exotic scent. She was wet and hot, begging to be tasted.

Bending forward, he licked at her sensitive pink flesh, enjoying the taste and texture. Katie thrashed about in the bed and grabbed a hank of hair to try and direct his actions more to her liking.

He blew softly on her heated skin before raising himself to stare at her flushed face. "Now, I'm going to eat you until you come." Katie's eyes widened for a moment and then she thrust her hips up to encourage him to get on with it.

Cain immediately took the hard nubbin of flesh into his mouth and sucked. His long, thick fingers glided along her moist, heated flesh before sliding inside her. Katie moaned and gripped the sheet in her hands. Cain could feel the sweat sliding down his back as he desperately tried to keep his control. His cock was close to exploding.

Katie was arching wildly now as he pumped his fingers in and out of her body. Her internal muscles clenched and grasped at his fingers. Cain's tentative control snapped. He wanted to be inside her when she came. No, he needed to be inside her. He wanted her body clenching his cock, not his fingers.

He withdrew his fingers and before Katie could object, he flipped her over onto her stomach again. Raising her slightly, he grabbed a pillow with the other hand and tucked it under her stomach. Her bottom was raised slightly in the air, but the pillow made the position more comfortable.

"Spread your legs and relax, honey," he whispered as he positioned himself on his knees behind her.

Katie eagerly spread her legs and arched her bottom towards him and he slid his cock right into her waiting warmth. He closed his eye and clenched his teeth, waiting for a wave of pleasure to pass. It was almost too much to take. Her inner muscles were squeezing him, in an exquisite form of sexual torture. His balls were tightening and he knew he only had a moment or two before he exploded.

Grasping her waist with his hands, he began to move within her. He plunged into her repeatedly. Her moans of pleasure spurred him to push harder and deeper. Katie responded by thrusting her bottom back towards him. The sound of her plump, juicy ass slapping his stomach made him even hotter.

Katie's breath hitched and her inner muscles clasped his cock in a warm, wet vise. It was the end for him as he felt himself come in a long, hot spurt. Her muscles clenched tighter and he could hear her wail of release. She thumped her feet on the bed and her fingers tore at the sheets. He continued to pump his hips for another moment, but he was totally drained and collapsed on top of her.

Cain knew he was squashing Katie, but he couldn't move. Her body continued to spasm around his cock and the pleasure was making him lightheaded. They lay there on the bed, both spent in a heap of wet, sweaty flesh. Never had Cain felt so utterly replete and relaxed in his life.

It was Katie squirming beneath him that finally gave him the motivation to move. Reluctantly, he pulled himself from her body, hissing as he did so. The sensation was as much pleasure and pain. He lay there for another moment and gathered the strength to roll from the bed.

Katie didn't move a muscle, her ass still pushed up into the air as she half-sat, half-lay on her knees. She lay with her legs still wide open, totally exposed to him, and he stopped for a moment to admire the pretty picture she made with her wet, pink pussy wide open to him. Her face was still buried in the pillow and the occasional shiver racked her body. A man could easily become addicted to this. Cain felt a smile of pure masculine satisfaction cover his face. He'd exhausted her with pleasure.

Cain went into the bathroom, flushed the condom and ran a cold, wet cloth over his body to cool his heated flesh. He dropped the wet cloth in the sink, leaned his hands on the counter, and stared at his reflection in the mirror. He looked different. It took him a moment to realize what that difference was. He looked like a man well content with his life.

For a moment, he was shaken by the thought that one woman could have such a hold on him and affect his life so much. Then he relaxed. Deep down inside, he trusted Katie not to use him or manipulate him. He honestly trusted her. Besides which, he reminded himself grimly, he'd had a taste of life without her and that was not an option he was willing to even contemplate.

Katie shivered, suddenly cold without Cain's large body covering her. Little aftershocks of desire pulsed through her and she squirmed on the mattress, enjoying the sensation. She was slightly appalled when she realized she was still wantonly sprawled on her stomach with her legs spread and her bottom stuck up in the air. No wonder she was cold. Marshaling her strength, she rolled over in bed, and shoved aside the tangle of sheets.

Rubbing her hands over her face, she stared at the bathroom door. Cain had been in there for quite a while. Worried, she climbed out of bed, pulling one of the sheets with her. Wrapping it around her, she padded silently to the bathroom. She peeked in through the open door. Cain had both hands planted on the counter and was glaring at himself in the mirror.

Taking advantage of the moment, her eyes feasted on his body. She licked her dry lips as she allowed her gaze to flow from the bottom of his feet to the top of his head. He had huge feet and strong, muscled calves and thighs. His taut bottom was a delicious sight and well, his penis was impressive, even when it was only partially aroused as it was now. His waist was thick with muscle, his chest was massive, and his arms the size of tree trunks. Cain looked large with his clothes on, but naked, she realized just what a massive specimen of manhood he was.

As if sensing her perusal, he turned and gave her a cocky half-smile. "Like what you see?"

"Very much," she teased back. She sauntered over to him and wrapped one arm around his waist and hugged him tight, burying her face in his back. Her fingers lightly skimmed the scarred part of his back. He shuddered but didn't stop her.

Emboldened, she traced the scars on his arm before bending forward to kiss them. Cain turned and wrapped her in his embrace.

"Katie," he began.

"I love all of you, you know," Katie murmured as she kissed his chest.

His arms tightened around her. "Thank you."

Katie knew that he loved her and someday he would say the words. Until he was ready, she was content with knowing it in her heart. Trying to lighten the moment she glanced around the bathroom and her gaze landed on the huge tub in the corner.

"I need a bath." She pulled away from Cain and headed towards the tub, the train of her sheet sweeping along behind her. Bending over she turned on the taps and adjusted the running water. "I came here straight from work and I feel grubby."

Cain slipped behind her and yanked at the sheet. A slight tug-of-war ensued, but in the end she lost. But he hadn't fought fair. He'd distracted her with kisses and when she'd reached out to wrap her arms around him, he'd whipped off the sheet and tossed it aside. Katie didn't really mind, even though she gave him a mock glare. She loved the sound of his laughter as they played.

Their lighthearted mood continued as they both settled into the tub. When the tub was filled to her satisfaction, Katie turned off the taps and settled back to allow the hot water to work their magic on her sore muscles. She splashed Cain with water and tried to push him under the water. Cain responded by actually dunking her head first. Water sloshed over the sides of the tub as they each battled for supremacy. Sputtering and promising dire retribution, she lunged at him, but he caught her easily in his arms and settled her on his lap facing him.

His hands shook as he pushed her wet hair off her forehead. Katie sensed the change in his mood. Without speaking, Cain picked up a soft cloth and soaped it before running it over her arms and her chest. He swirled the cloth around her sensitive breasts and Katie felt the passion begin to grow in her again.

"That feels so good." Katie encouraged him and was rewarded when the soapy cloth slid around her back and over her bottom. Cain really seemed to like her behind. He dropped the cloth and squeezed both globes in his wet hands.

Using his hands, he rinsed the soap from her breasts. She could feel his arousal between her legs and reached under the water and guided him inside her. The soapy water and her own arousal ensured that he slid right in. Both of them moaned with pleasure, as their sensitive flesh joined again.

Cain gripped her hips and held her tight. Neither of them moved, both content just to be joined together. Katie's breasts swayed slightly as her breathing became more labored. Cain's gaze heated and he bent his knees so that her back was supported and the movement pushed her breasts closer to his waiting mouth.

This time, their lovemaking was tender and unhurried. Cain nipped and nibbled her breasts while his hands continued to explore her back, her bottom, her thighs, and finally her waiting clitoris. Katie was just as busy as she mapped out the glistening muscles of his back and his chest. She played with his nipples before reaching behind her to gently squeeze and fondle his balls. Slowly, she rocked up and down on his rock-hard erection.

Her release when it came was slower, deeper, and somehow more satisfying than ever before. Cain retained some measure of control as he pulled out of her at the last minute and she pumped her hand up and down his cock so that he came in the water instead of inside her. It was his way of looking out for her and taking care of her.

Reluctantly, Katie climbed from the bath. She wanted to loll about in the water, but didn't think that was a good idea. Stepping on the plush bathmat, Katie watched Cain clean himself up while she toweled off. He quickly soaped himself from head to toe and immersed himself under water before rising like some giant sea serpent. Give him a pitchfork and he'd look like Poseidon, she thought.

Hauling himself from the tub, he grabbed a towel and briskly rubbed himself dry. He caught her staring at him and swept her up in his arms and carried her from the bathroom and back to the bed. Still holding her in his arms, he fell backwards onto the bed and then rolled so that she was under him.

Her eyes widened as she felt his growing arousal again. "That's impossible," she informed him.

"Not with you around," he informed her smugly. He rubbed his penis against her mound and grinned when she opened her legs and arched against him.

He was lowering his lips to hers when her stomach gave a huge unladylike grumble. Cain just leaned back and stared at her stomach. Katie was thoroughly disgruntled by his expression of amazement and her rumbling tummy.

"Well, what do you expect?" she groused. "You're always promising me supper, but never feeding me." She glanced at the bedside table. "It's almost midnight and I haven't had a bite to eat since about half past eleven this morning. And that was just a single cinnamon bun."

"We can't let you starve. I've got a long night planned so we better keep your strength up." Cain planted a hard, quick kiss on her lips and pulled himself out of bed. He crossed to the armoire and pulled out a pair of sweatpants and tugged them on.

Glancing back towards the bed, he tossed her one of his old denim shirts. "If you don't cover up, I'll never let you eat."

Katie just smiled seductively and tugged on his shirt over her damp body. Cain just shook his head and crossed back to the bed. "You are one dangerous lady. Now be good while I go forage for some food."

Buttoning the shirt, Katie burrowed under the covers and eagerly awaited Cain's return.

Katie felt totally satisfied. Curled up next to Cain in the dark of the night, enveloped in his warmth and the safety of his arms, Katie knew she'd finally found where she belonged. True to his word, Cain had indeed fed her. He'd returned from the kitchen with a feast of cheese, crackers, fruit, and meat. A bottle of white wine had complemented their impromptu picnic. Gabriel had snuck in and managed to con them out of a few pieces of cheese, but when no more food was forthcoming, he gave a big doggy huff and retreated from the room.

They had eaten with abandon, feeding each other tasty morsels of food, and sharing a single glass of wine. Both of them had been starving, and so they finished every bite of food he'd carried into the bedroom. When nothing but crumbs remained, Cain had turned his attention back to her.

Katie smiled and snuggled closer as she remembered their lovemaking. That last time had been more playful. Both of them were comfortable and completely at home with one another. They had feasted on each other. Taking turns and romping in the bed like inquisitive nymphs. Well, she was the nymph, he was more of a satyr. But like her, he was now a well-pleased one.

As if sensing she was awake, Cain pulled her tighter towards him and groaned when she playfully wiggled her behind against his partial erection.

"You're a wicked woman, Katie." Leisurely, he kissed her ear, his tongue swirling around the outer shell.

Katie moaned and cuddled closer. Cain tucked her head under his chin and sighed contentedly. Both of them lay there for a long time, neither one speaking, both of them satisfied with just being together.

Cain finally broke the silence. "I've thought about Lucas's situation." Katie stiffened in his arms, but didn't speak. "I can't change the plans already in place for the building he's in, but I can help him find another location, one he can afford with a silent partner."

Katie couldn't believe Cain's generosity. "Thank you, Cain. Your offer means a lot, but I think Lucas will want to do this on his own." Turning in his arms she kissed his cheek. "Everything will all work out."

Cain pulled her back into his arms. This time, he settled her so that her head was pillowed on his chest. Happily, she nuzzled his skin and dozed as the sound of his heartbeat comforted her.

"I love you." His voice was a hoarse whisper in the darkness.

Katie could hear the sincerity and love in his voice. She bit her lip to keep herself from crying, knowing how hard it was for him to actually say the words. "I know," she replied in a low voice.

Cain tensed next to her and then he laughed. "You little minx. What do you mean, you know?"

Katie had to sit up when he started laughing. It was impossible to rest when your pillow kept jiggling. "It was obvious by your actions even if you didn't say the word."

Cain rolled over and tucked her beneath him. "What do you have to say for yourself?"

Unconcerned by his mock ferocity, she took her time and settled herself comfortably on the pillows. When he continued to scowl at her, she just grinned back at him. "I love you too."

"Damn it, Katie." Cain leaned down and plundered her mouth. His lips, teeth, and tongue teased and pleasured her. The kiss went on and on, as if Cain craved the connection between them. Katie's head was spinning when he finally withdrew from her lips. "Thank you for bringing me out of the dark."

Katie responded the only way she could. "Thank you for showing me the beauty of the dark." Cain's arms tightened around her and Katie reached for him, determined to love him. Forever.

Epilogue

"I'm home." Katie closed the door behind her and kicked off her boots. In the last month she'd probably spent as much time here as she had in her own apartment. If Cain had it his way, she'd have moved in with him. Hanging up her coat and purse, Katie paused to straighten her sweater. She was getting closer to making a decision, but it was hard to think of giving up the only home she'd ever known.

The sound of toenails was her only warning before Gabriel bounded up behind her and jumped. Now that she had become a regular part of his life, the dog no longer felt the need to be always on his best behavior. "Get down, you brute," she scolded him mockingly even as she began to tussle with him.

They played in the hallway for a few minutes and Katie was surprised when Cain didn't appear. He was usually right there to greet her when she arrived from work. Giving the dog one final pat, she began her search. "Cain?"

"In here." His voice drifted out from the office.

She and Gabriel hurried down the hallway, and Gabriel ran into the room ahead of her. Katie halted in the doorway, amazed by the sight in front of her. Cain was standing in front of a large six-foot square canvas that was set tilted against one wall and surrounded at its base by drop cloths. He was naked from the waist up, with his arms crossed over his massive chest. His bare feet were spread slightly as he stood atop the canvas cloth on the floor. A table had been set up next to the canvas and was filled with what looked like paints and brushes. Bemused, she headed towards Cain. "Have you decided to take up painting?"

"In a manner of speaking." His enigmatic reply piqued her interest.

"That's a rather large canvas you're planning to fill." Her fingers were itching to pick up a brush and use it. The sheer freedom in having such an expansive work area was enticing.

"You can help me." His voice was rough and compelling and, as usual, she fell under its spell.

Katie's gaze moved from the blank canvas to Cain. His long black hair was pulled away from his face and tied at the nape of his neck. The black eye patch seemed to emphasize the harsh planes of his face, and his good eye had that special gleam it usually had when he was aroused. Her eyes traced a path down over his wide shoulders and muscled stomach towards the bulge in his jeans. Yep, he was certainly aroused.

Feeling rather hot, she unbuttoned her sweater and slipped it off her shoulders as she sauntered towards him. "I can help you later," she whispered seductively as she ran her hands up his hard stomach and wrapped her arms around his neck. Pressing her partially naked torso against his chest, she nipped at his neck and chin.

Cain's fingers lightly skimmed her back before unhooking the back closure of her bra. She was forced to remove her arms long enough to allow him to pull her bra down her arms. When it was gone, she lightly rubbed her breasts across his chest, loving the feel of his hot skin against hers.

"I want you to help me now." His hands were tugging at the opening of her jeans, so it took her a moment for his words to sink in.

Slightly disgruntled, she leaned back and looked at him with disbelief. "You want to paint now?"

In answer, he knelt on one knee in front of her, pulled her jeans and underwear down to her ankles, and waited while she stepped out of them. "Oh, yes. I definitely want to paint now." Cain kissed her stomach, his moist tongue dipping into her belly button while his palms traced upward along the back of her thighs until they cupped her behind.

Holding his shoulders for balance, she studied his intent expression, trying to understand his unusual mood. "If that's what you *really* want." It wasn't what she desired at the moment, but if Cain wanted to share in her passion for painting, she was more than ready to participate.

Cain led her to the table. "Stand here."

Slightly bewildered, she wondered what she was doing standing here naked while Cain opened up bottles of paint and squirted colors onto a blank palette. "Am I to be your model?" It had finally occurred to her that he might want to paint her nude.

"In a manner of speaking." Taking his time, he selected a large brush with a blunt tip and dipped it into the red paint. He moved in front of her and tilted his head to one side and looked her up and down. Katie could feel her skin smoldering under his scrutiny, and her nipples contracted into hard nubs. Smiling slightly, he used his free hand to position her hands on her hips. "Spread your legs a little more."

Katie complied and then stood still, knowing that it was important to an artist that the subject not move around too much. Her gaze went to the canvas as she wondered where Cain would start his painting. The sudden shock of bristles moving across her breasts made her take a step back. Looking down at herself, she could see the stroke of red paint covering her distended nipple.

"You've got to stand still." When she looked at him, Cain was frowning at her. "How can I paint you if you're moving?"

Katie took a better look at the paints on the table, and the words "Body Paint" were written boldly across all the tubes. Cain looked so serious standing there, waiting impatiently, that she burst out laughing. Bending over, she clasped her stomach as she laughed even harder. Cain looked totally disgruntled as he waited for her to finish. When she subsided to just giggles, Cain repositioned her with her hands on her hips and her legs spread.

"Don't move." Cain waited until she'd nodded her agreement before beginning again.

Like a master painter, he took his time and selected his colors carefully. He returned to the red paint and slowly, meticulously painted both her breasts red. The feel of the delicate fan-shaped bristles caressing her skin was unbelievable arousing. She unconsciously swayed towards the brush as he worked.

Next came the orange. With a flat-headed, camelhair brush, he applied long stripes of the cheerful color to her stomach. The bristles tickled her sides, making her shake with laughter. Cain raised his head, and the tender look in his eye almost moved her to tears. Their love had given him the freedom and comfort to allow him to play, and Katie would stand here all night long if it made him happy.

Sap green was the next color of choice. Using a small housepainter's brush, he coated her legs from ankle to thigh. Moving behind her, he kissed a trail up her back before applying, first yellow ochre, and then ultramarine in a swirling pattern. He took his time on her behind, making her squirm as the brush moved back and forth over the cleft of her bottom. She was so aroused that she could feel the wetness between her legs and a throbbing ache that longed to be filled.

"Cain, hurry and finish." Squirming slightly as he continued to paint her bottom violet, she started to turn around, but he stopped her.

"Soon," he promised.

Returning to her front he picked up a clean fan brush and tested the bristles between his fingers. She wanted those fingers inside her, filling her. The image was potent and she reached out to him, wanting him desperately. She felt almost dizzy with desire.

"Just a little longer," he crooned as he moved her hands back to her waist. Before she could protest, he positioned himself on his knees in front of her, slid the brush between her legs, and brushed the sensitive skin of her sex.

"Oh, god," she moaned and opened her legs wider.

"That's it," he encouraged. "So pretty and pink already, but I think I'll add just a touch more." The brush glided over the folds of her sex, tickling and arousing her at the same time. Taking a small liner brush, he plied it with skill around and around her clitoris until she was sweating and begging him to take her.

"Now, Cain." She didn't move her hands from her side, but placed one foot on the top of his shoulder. The position left her wide open to him, and she moved her hips invitingly.

Cain wrapped one arm around her waist to steady her as he grabbed another clean brush with a rounded thick set of bristles. Slowly, he fitted it inside her, swirling it from side to side as he went. Katie had never experienced anything like this in her life and would have collapsed if Cain hadn't been supporting her.

Giving herself over to the experience, she flexed her hips, taking the brush deeper inside her. Cain pushed it as far in as was comfortable and then removed it with one long, pleasurable stroke to the top of her vagina. Sensation shot through her all the way from her toes to her head. She came immediately, unable to control the sudden explosion inside her. Screaming slightly she collapsed and Cain quickly dropped the brush and lowered her to the floor.

When she finally came back to herself, Cain was leaning over her, grinning like a fool. One hand was idly stroking her heated flesh with his fingers. "So, you're finger-painting now?" The question popped out of her mouth before she could stop herself. Cain burst into laughter and collapsed on the floor next to her.

Grinning, she took advantage of Cain's momentary distraction to rise up next to him and unbutton his jeans. Before he could stop her, she got to her feet and tugged his jeans and underwear down his legs and threw them aside. "Now it's my turn." She fisted her hands on her waist and waited, praying that he'd give up control to her. It was still hard for him to do so, but she did need her way sometimes.

Cain surprised her by making himself comfortable on the canvas drop cloth and stacking his hands underneath his head. "You're the painter."

"I certainly am," she agreed. Having his magnificent body presented to her to do exactly as she pleased was a huge turn-on. With her own body still thrumming contently after her explosive orgasm, she set about to return the favor to Cain.

Taking a small round brush, she dipped it in indigo paint and sat on his stomach. With her legs spread on either side of his chest, her sex was wide open on him. Taking a moment, she shimmied around until she was comfortable, then she began to paint.

The hardest thing he'd ever done was to lie passive on the floor and let her do whatever she wanted to him. He clasped his hands tight behind his head, and his arms corded with muscle as he kept himself still. He could feel her pussy spreading its wetness on his chest, he wanted to throw her on her back and just spend the next hour pounding into her. His cock felt like it was going to explode any minute, so he distracted himself by silently reciting the details of a contract he'd signed today.

Taken off-guard, he flinched when she moved the brush towards his face. She ignored it and started to paint the right side of his face in indigo. He held himself rigid as she worked her way down his face and neck to his chest.

"You'll look like a barbarian king when I'm finished," she promised.

Cain didn't care how he looked as long as she hurried. His endurance was stretched to the limit and he didn't know how much longer he could allow her to paint him.

Fortunately for both of them, Katie was a professional and wasn't trying to cover his whole body like he did to her. It was as if she sensed he was near the end of his rope, and it was already frayed. Working in the dark blue, she continued to paint a swirling, slightly Celtic design down his torso, over his thighs and calves, finally finishing at his ankles. The slight scratch of the brush against the hair of his chest and legs was incredibly stimulating. His cock jerked and throbbed begging him to do something. Immediately.

Gritting his teeth, he swallowed hard and waited to see what Katie would do. Cleaning her brush, she returned to sit on the tops of his thighs. "Katie." It was a request and an order. She had to touch him.

Wielding the brush with care, she swept the length of his dick from the base to the tip. He almost came when she swirled the brush around the tip. Several drops of arousal leaked out of the top and she dipped her brush in it and "painted" her way back down to the base. His testicles were tight against his body and drew even tighter as she brushed his scrotum, taking care to sweep the creases at the top of his thighs.

Cain was enthralled at the picture she made, sitting on him like some naked fairy queen. Painted from the neck down, she was a huge splash of color. Her red breasts swayed as she worked and he was mesmerized by them, wanting no more then to take them into his mouth. He promised himself then that next time he'd find edible paints. Her orange torso and green legs made a perfect frame for the hot, pink flesh between her legs.

The brush flicked the tip of his erection and he erupted into action. Before she knew what was happening, Cain flipped her onto her back and drove into her in one long stroke. She reached her arms up to him, but he jerked away. "I don't want to smear the paint yet," he gritted out.

Katie spread her arms out at her sides and gripped the cloth between her fingers. God, he loved this woman, she pleased him like no other, understanding his needs and his moods almost better than he did himself.

On his knees in front of her, he pulled her close so that her thighs were draped over his, and lifted her legs around his waist. She immediately locked her feet behind his back drawing him even further inside her. The heat surrounding his cock was incredible and a groan of pleasure slipped from him.

Wanting to watch her come again, he used his fingers to spread the top part of her sex open, exposing her totally. Lightly, he played his fingers across her clitoris.

"Harder, Cain," Katie pleaded.

He pressed it harder as he began to move inside her again. At first, the strokes were slow and even, but that didn't last long. Needing to thrust harder, Cain reluctantly removed his fingers and wrapped his hands around her waist. Levering himself up slightly, he began to thrust hard. His strokes became deeper as he hammered into her.

He could feel her inner muscles clamping around his cock even as he felt himself explode inside of her. Cain came hard and long inside of her, his hot semen spurted deep inside her until there was nothing left inside him. He heard Katie's scream of release as she came and he closed his eye, letting his head to fall back and allowing the feeling of completion to wash over him.

Swallowing hard, he tipped his head forward and opened his eye. Katie was lying motionless on the floor with her eyes closed, arms flung out by her sides, and her legs sprawled wide open with him still inside her. Smiling at the totally debauched picture she made, he slowly withdrew from her. Grumbling slightly, she opened one eye and glared at him.

"Time to get up." He staggered to his feet and offered her his hand. She stared at him as if he was out of his mind. "It's time to paint."

"I'm doing this under protest," she told him as she took his hand and allowed him to pull her to her feet.

"I'll have you cleaned up and tucked in bed in no time," he promised. "But first, I want a painting of us."

Leading her to the large canvas, he backed her up against the white sheet and pressed her backwards so that her legs, bottom, and back were against the canvas. Slowly, he turned her, rolling her along the canvas until her breasts and the fronts of her arms and legs were now pressed against it.

A muffled laugh came from her. "You're crazy." But she was into the spirit of the project and pushed her arms against the paper. "You've got to do it too."

Cain let go of her and moved to a clear spot and leaned into the canvas. He turned his body from side to side until he figured there was a good impression and stepped back. The pattern of indigo was visible. "Not bad."

Katie was standing next to him, grinning widely. Paint was smeared across her body, her hair was standing on end, and there was a smudge of blue on her cheek.

Reaching over, his thumb swiped at the paint, but ended up only adding to the mess.

Katie stood on her toes and pulled his head down so that she could reach him. Tenderly, she placed a kiss on his ravaged cheek before moving to his lips. "Thank you." She didn't say for what, but they both knew. He had trusted her enough to relinquish some of his control to her, share his body openly, and show his playful side.

"Just don't get used to it," he responded gruffly as he scooped her into his arms. A whine from the corner had him turning with Katie tight in his grasp. Gabriel was lying safely in the corner with his paw over his eyes.

"I guess we were too much for his doggy sensibilities," Katie said laughingly.

"I love you, Katie." Cain's voice was thick with emotion as he spoke. She had changed his life so much by accepting his darkness while sharing her light and laughter with him.

"I love you, too." Snuggling her head on his chest, she wrapped her arms trustingly around his neck and placed a kiss by his heart. Cain wrapped her even tighter in his embrace and carried her from the room, smearing the paint on their two bodies together where they touched.

The picture against the wall was no masterpiece, but it was indeed a testament to their love. The dark blue of his outline was a stark contrast to the vibrant colors of Katie, but somehow they looked right together, felt right together. Just like him and Katie. Cain planned to have it hung tomorrow.

Enjoy this excerpt from

Erin's Fancy

Awakening Desires

© Copyright N.J. Walters, 2005

Erin Connors ran her index finger over the glossy magazine cover with the scantily clad cover model and underlined the article "Seven Sex Positions That Will Drive You Both Wild!"

Taking a deep breath, she opened the cover and scanned the table of contents. She flipped through the pages, stopping at, appropriately enough, page sixty-nine, and spread the magazine wide on the scarred wood table in front of her. Bold pink letters flashed up at her from the page: *Legs on shoulders, Doggy-style, Sixty-nine, Standing Backward Position, Face-to-Face, Spooning and Scissors.* She could feel the heat creeping up her face as she perused the pictures of half-naked couples, with strategically placed clothing and blankets, demonstrating the techniques.

Glancing up, she peeked out the open back door and noted that the yard was empty. Her brother Jackson was busy in the barn and Nathan had already left for work. The coast was clear. Sighing, she rubbed the back of her suntanned neck. It was pathetic that a woman of twenty-five had to hide the fact that she was reading a woman's magazine. Especially a magazine that gave advice about sex. That's what came from still living at home at her age, and having two, very large, very protective older brothers, one of whom was a local deputy sheriff. They still treated her like some kind of nun who supposedly never even thought about sex, much less had sex.

That was entirely the problem. She hadn't had sex. Well, technically she had, but she didn't count graduation night in the back of Brad Hutchinson's pick-up truck out at Peak's Pond. That had been a lot of fumbling, a little pain, and a whole lot of nothing! It had been such a disaster that Erin had never quite worked up the nerve to try it again. Not that she'd had much of an opportunity.

The fact of the matter was that men didn't notice her. Well, they noticed her, but not for the right reasons. Erin was what was known as "a big girl." Six feet tall in her stocking feet, her arms and legs muscular, and her shoulders wide from working side-by-side with her brothers tended to be off-putting to a lot of men.

It wouldn't have been so bad, but the only part of her that wasn't large was her breasts. She'd gotten shortchanged in that department. Though nicely rounded, they tended to disappear in the overalls and loose shirts she wore for work.

Still, she wasn't ugly. Her hair was deep auburn, but it was a thick, curly mess that wouldn't hold a style, so she usually kept it confined in a single braid that fell to her waist. She had the Connor blue eyes, the pale blue of a sunny summer sky, just like her brothers Jackson and Nathan. Her nose tilted up just slightly and had a light dusting of freckles, and her lips were wide and full. It was a nice face, a comfortable face, and that was part of the problem.

Erin looked like the proverbial girl-next-door with her wholesome looks. Tagging behind her older brothers, doing the same work, had quickly labeled her a tomboy. By the time she'd become interested in what it meant to be a girl, everyone was used to her being just one of the guys. None of the girls in the neighborhood or at school had liked her because she was a friend to all the boys. Conversely, all the guys liked her because she didn't act like a girl.

The problem was that when all the boys grew into men and the girls grew into women, Erin was left out. The men started dating and she was still just one of the boys. Everybody's pal, that was her. And she hated it. Maybe not all of it. But damn it, she was a woman too, with women's needs, except no one ever seemed to notice. If she was ever to get the sweaty, grinding, orgasmic sex that she wanted, she needed help.

Turning her attention to the article, she began to read aloud: "Any man who's being truthful will tell you his favorite position is doggy style. It's very primal and sexy to your man." Okay, she'd grown up in a farming community, so she could understand the animalistic appeal to a guy.

"Just get down on all fours and stick your ass in the air. No, it's not the most dignified position in the world." Erin pictured it in her head and thought that this was an understatement. In fact, she figured it would look pretty ridiculous, but what did she know. These people were the experts or they never would have gotten published in this magazine.

As her eyes drifted closed, the image in her head changed slightly and came into sharper focus. She saw herself kneeling on the kitchen linoleum with her face pressed to the cool floor and her ass stuck up in the air. A man stood behind her, but she couldn't quite picture his features, but his deep voice washed over her, filling her with pleasure...

"Spread your legs wider and offer yourself to me."

Erin could feel her juices run down her legs as she slid her knees as far apart as they would go. She could feel the heat rolling off of him as he knelt behind her. Without warning, he gripped her hips with his large hands and thrust his cock deep inside her. Moaning, she ground her bottom against him. He laughed and slipped his hands up to cup her breasts. "You know you want me to fuck you, don't you?"

"Yes," she cried. "Fuck me. Hard." He began pumping into her from behind.

Erin's eyes popped open and she gasped for breath, desperately trying to focus on the magazine page in front of her.

Grabbing her tall glass of ice tea, she took a huge gulp and continued to read. "We guarantee he'll go crazy. As he enters you from behind, he'll go in very deep and will hit your G-spot. He can also stimulate your breasts and clitoris in this position." She paused to take a deep breath.

"He most certainly can," she panted. Her underwear was wet and she could feel her inner muscles contracting slightly. She wasn't even sure where her G-spot was, but she was certainly feeling hot. The glass was sweaty and cool, and she rubbed it against her cheeks and neck. It made her feel slightly better.

About the author:

N. J. Walters had a mid-life crisis at a fairly young age, gave notice after ten years at her job on a Friday, received a tentative acceptance for her first novel, Annabelle Lee, on the following Sunday.

Happily married for over seventeen years to the love of her life, with his encouragement and support she gave up the job of selling books for the more pleasurable job of writing them. A voracious reader of romances of all kinds, she now spends her days writing, reading and reviewing books. It's a tough life, but someone's got to do it.

N.J. Walters welcomes mail from readers. You can write to her c/o Ellora's Cave Publishing at 1056 Home Ave. Akron, Oh. 44310-3502.

Why an electronic book?

We live in the Information Age—an exciting time in the history of human civilization in which technology rules supreme and continues to progress in leaps and bounds every minute of every hour of every day. For a multitude of reasons, more and more avid literary fans are opting to purchase e-books instead of paperbacks. The question to those not yet initiated to the world of electronic reading is simply: *why?*

1. *Price.* An electronic title at Ellora's Cave Publishing and Cerridwen Press runs anywhere from 40-75% less than the cover price of the <u>exact same title</u> in paperback format. Why? Cold mathematics. It is less expensive to publish an e-book than it is to publish a paperback, so the savings are passed along to the consumer.

2. *Space.* Running out of room to house your paperback books? That is one worry you will never have with electronic novels. For a low one-time cost, you can purchase a handheld computer designed specifically for e-reading purposes. Many e-readers are larger than the average handheld, giving you plenty of screen room. Better yet, hundreds of titles can be stored within your new library—a single microchip. (Please note that Ellora's Cave and Cerridwen Press does not endorse any specific brands. You can check our website at www.ellorascave.com or

www.cerridwenpress.com for customer recommendations we make available to new consumers.)

3. *Mobility.* Because your new library now consists of only a microchip, your entire cache of books can be taken with you wherever you go.

4. *Personal preferences are accounted for.* Are the words you are currently reading too small? Too large? Too…**ANNOYING**? Paperback books cannot be modified according to personal preferences, but e-books can.

5. *Instant gratification.* Is it the middle of the night and all the bookstores are closed? Are you tired of waiting days—sometimes weeks—for online and offline bookstores to ship the novels you bought? Ellora's Cave Publishing sells instantaneous downloads 24 hours a day, 7 days a week, 365 days a year. Our e-book delivery system is 100% automated, meaning your order is filled as soon as you pay for it.

Those are a few of the top reasons why electronic novels are displacing paperbacks for many an avid reader. As always, Ellora's Cave and Cerridwen Press welcomes your questions and comments. We invite you to email us at service@ellorascave.com, service@cerridwenpress.com or write to us directly at: 1056 Home Ave. Akron OH 44310-3502.

NEED A MORE EXCITING
WAY TO PLAN YOUR DAY?

ELLORA'S
CAVEMEN

2006 CALENDAR

COMING THIS FALL

THE
ELLORA'S CAVE
LIBRARY

Stay up to date with Ellora's Cave Titles
in Print with our Quarterly Catalog.

To recieve a catalog,
send an email with your name
and mailing address to:

CATALOG@ELLORASCAVE.COM

or send a letter or postcard
with your mailing address to:

Catalog Request
c/o Ellora's Cave Publishing, Inc.
1337 Commerce Drive #13
Stow, OH 44224

Lady Jaided

The premier magazine for today's sensual woman

Lady Jaided magazine is devoted to exploring the sexuality and sensuality of women. While there are many similarities between the sexual experiences of men and women, there are just as many if not more differences. Our focus is on the female experience and on giving voice and credence to it. Lady Jaided will include everything from trends, politics, science and history to gossip, humor and celebrity interviews, but our focus will remain on female sexuality and sensuality.

A Sneak Peek at Upcoming Stories

Clan of the Cave Woman
Women's sexuality throughout history.

The Sarandon Syndrome
What's behind the attraction between older women and younger men.

The Last Taboo
Why some women – even feminists – have bondage fantasies

Girls' Eyes for Queer Guys
An in-depth look at the attraction between straight women and gay men

Available Spring 2005

Lady *Jaided* Regular Features

Jaid's Tirade

Jaid Black's erotic romance novels sell throughout the world, and her publishing company Ellora's Cave is one of the largest and most successful e-book publishers in the world. What is less well known about Jaid Black, a.k.a. Tina Engler is her long record as a political activist. Whether she's discussing sex or politics (or both), expect to see her get up on her soapbox and do what she does best: offend the greedy, the holier-than-thous, and the apathetic! Don't miss out on her monthly column.

Devilish Dot's G-Spot

Married to the same man for 20 years, Dorothy Araiza still basks in a sex life to be envied. What Dot loves just as much as achieving the Big O is helping other women realize their full sexual potential. Dot gives talks and advice on everything from which sex toys to buy (or not to buy) to which positions give you the best climax.

On the Road with Lady K

Publisher, author, world traveler and Lady of Barrow, Kathryn Falk shares insider information on the most romantic places in the world.

Kandidly Kay

This Lois Lane cum Dave Barry is a domestic goddess by day and a hard-hitting sexual deviancy reporter by night. Adored for her stunning wit and knack for delivering one-liners, this Rodney Dangerfield of reporting will leave no stone unturned in her search for the bizarre truth.

A Model World

CJ Hollenbach returns to his roots. The blond heartthrob from Ohio has twice been seen in Playgirl magazine and countless other publications. He has appeared on several national TV shows including The Jerry Springer Show (God help him!) and has been interviewed for Entertainment Tonight, CNN and The Today Show. He has been involved in the romance industry for the past 12 years, appearing on dozens of romance novel covers and calendars. CJ's specialty is personal interviews, in which people have a tendency to tell him everything.

Hot Mama Cooks

Sex is her food, and food is her sex. Hot Mama gives aphrodisiac a whole new meaning. Join her every month for her latest sensual adventure -- with bonus recipe!

Empress on the Mount

Brash, outrageous, and undeniably irreverent, this advice columnist from down under will either leave you in stitches or recovering from hang-jaw as you gawk at her answers to reader questions on relationships and life.

Erotic Fiction from Ellora's Cave

The debut issue will feature part one of "Ferocious," a three-part erotic serial written especially for Lady Jaided by the popular Sherri L. King.